"You don't know how beautiful you are," he softly told her. "You don't know how much I think about you."

"Jake." His name was a whisper. A sigh. A promise. She tipped her chin up and watched him with glittering eyes that were already half-closed, surrendering even as she continued to fight. "I thought we agreed we weren't going to do this."

Reaching up, mesmerized by everything about this one special woman, he smoothed the wet hair past her temple. Traced one silky brow. Ran his thumb across the dewy velvet of her lower lip.

"I've been trying." He shrugged helplessly. "I didn't know how hard it would be."

Leaning in, he dipped his head and, making sure to keep their bodies well apart, kissed her before she could protest—one gentle, lingering, perfect kiss that nearly choked him with desire.

Then he pulled back, knowing he'd crossed a line but unable to remember why that should matter.

Her eyes were bright and glazed now, a vivid mixture of gray and green that should only belong to the finest jewels and sunset-streaked oceans.

"You're so beautiful," he said again, shaking his head because life was unfair. Why else would God drop this woman in his life and then make her off-limits? "So beautiful."

"So are you."

Books by Ann Christopher

Kimani Romance

Just About Sex
Sweeter Than Revenge
Tender Secrets
Road to Seduction
Campaign for Seduction
Redemption's Kiss
Seduced on the Red Carpet
Redemption's Touch
The Surgeon's Secret Baby
Sinful Seduction
Sinful Temptation
Case for Seduction

ANN CHRISTOPHER

is a full-time chauffeur for her two overscheduled children. She is also a wife, former lawyer and decent cook. In between trips to various sporting practices and games, Target and the grocery store, she likes to write the occasional romance novel. She lives in Cincinnati and spends her time with her family, which includes two spoiled rescue cats, Sadie and Savannah, and two rescue hounds, Sheldon and Dexter. As always, Ann is hard at work on her next book.

If you'd like to recommend a great book, share a recipe for homemade cake of any kind or suggest a tip for getting your children to do what you say the *first* time you say it, Ann would love to hear from you through her website, www.AnnChristopher.com.

Case
for
Seduction
Ann Christopher

HARLEQUIN®
entertain, enrich, inspire™

To Richard

Recycling programs
for this product may
not exist in your area.

ISBN-13: 978-0-373-86273-3

CASE FOR SEDUCTION

Printed in U.S.A.

Dear Reader,

Are you ready to read about the Laws of Love? I sure hope so!

The Hamilton family is at the heart of this miniseries. The Hamiltons are wealthy and sexy Philadelphians, and almost all of the younger generation are lawyers working at Hamilton, Hamilton and Clark, the family's law firm.

And what happens when you throw family and lawyers together?

Emotions seethe. Oversized egos collide. Resentments boil over.

In other words, expect D-R-A-M-A, and plenty of it.

First up? My contribution to the series, *Case for Seduction*, where Jake Hamilton, who loves the ladies, meets his match in the form of his new paralegal, Charlotte Evans, a woman who's been right under his nose for years. Is Jake ready to be crazy in love? Absolutely not. That's what makes it so fun!

Next is Pamela Yaye's *Evidence of Desire*. You won't want to miss seeing Harper Hamilton fall—and fall hard—for Azure Ellison, the beautiful reporter who was formerly an ugly duckling at Harper's prep school. He never noticed her then, but, boy, is he making up for it now!

And the finale? Jacquelin Thomas's *Legal Attraction*, where Marissa Hamilton, the baby of the group, must deal with explosive family secrets and the fallout from her night of passion with her coworker and good friend Griff Jackson. What's the backdrop for all this tension, you ask? The family's glittering charity ball, of course....

So, buckle your seat belts. You're in for some exciting stories!

Happy reading!

Ann

Special thanks to Maria Ribas
and the team at Harlequin. It's always a pleasure.

Chapter 1

Jake Hamilton left the gym and ducked into Starbucks with one pressing question on his mind: Did they have any pumpkin scones left?

Having begun this fine September Saturday morning by working his butt off lifting weights, and then playing a squash match (he won, 3-0, thank you very much), he figured he was entitled to one of his favorite treats, even if he was a little…fragrant at the moment. Skirting the people in line, he peered into the glass display case, his hopes high.

Yes, he had a sweet tooth. He had about thirty-two of them, to be honest.

So, let's see. They have quite the selection this morning, don't they? Muffins…apple fritters…the usual as-

*sortment of cake slices—iced gingerbread, iced lemon
and chocolate—but no pumpkin scones, damn it.*

He scowled and made his way to the end of the line,
his morning ruined. Well, not entirely ruined, because
he could still get a gallon-sized cup of coffee, but it just
wouldn't be the same.

"Morning, Jake." The last of the customers in front
of him got their drinks and moved aside, revealing the
pretty barista behind the counter. She'd been making
eyes at him the last several times he was there, and he
felt terrible for not knowing her name by now. Trying
to be discreet, he checked her badge. *Ashley,* it said. "I
saved the last one for you. I figured you'd be needing
it." She held up a pumpkin scone on a plate.

Torn, Jake worked up a grin that he hoped wasn't
too enthusiastic. On the one hand, thank God he'd get
his scone. On the other hand, Ashley was now giving
him a quick once-over that stripped away the shorts and
T-shirt he was wearing and, while it was always flat-
tering to be noticed, he had no desire to be noticed by
Ashley.

Or by most of the females he encountered these days,
come to think of it, which was strange. He'd gotten to
the unfamiliar point in his life where he preferred to
sit quietly and alone in his house, watching ESPN and
prepping for his latest trial, instead of hanging out with
his brothers and catching the panties women threw their
way. The whole club scene had started to exhaust him.
The drinks. The dancing. The hookups. The aftermath,
which was always awkward to one degree or another.

When had he lost his taste for women who were young, beautiful and eager?

Why would he rather go sit at a table and organize his thoughts for the staff barbecue he was hosting at his house in a few weeks than stand here and flirt with Ashley?

Something was wrong with him, clearly.

But that was no reason to be rude.

"Thanks, Ashley." Extending his hand across the counter to accept the scone on its plate, he pretended he didn't feel the lingering brush of her fingers against his. "You just kept my day from turning into a disaster."

"Well." She preened as she fixed his coffee, tossing her shiny brown hair over one shoulder and giving him a smile that promised the sun, moon, stars and a ham sandwich if he crooked his little finger at her. "You owe me, don't you?"

"Absolutely," he told her, keeping his expression pleasant but distant and his little finger uncrooked. He reached into his pocket, grabbed a bill—it was a ten, alas, but oh, well; he'd chalk it up to money well spent— and handed it to her. "Thanks. Keep the change."

He turned away, aware of her faltering grin, and headed for a table in the most distant corner available, close to the window. He'd just set down his breakfast and was about to pull out a chair and sit, when it hit him: he'd forgotten to pick up copies of *The New York Times* and the *Philadelphia Daily News* while he was up at the counter.

He'd have to go back.

Unfortunately.

He wheeled around, determined to make it quick, while Ashley was restocking the cream and whatnot and— *Shit*.

He plowed straight into someone.

That someone hit the floor with a nasty thud.

Books went flying. A cappuccino mug and saucer shattered with a wet splatter, sending hot coffee in all directions. A slice of lemon cake skittered across the tiles and came to a stop beneath his table. Every head in the place swiveled in their direction.

"Sorry," he began automatically, his cheeks ablaze with embarrassment. Way to go, Hamilton. Why not just drive a backhoe through the plate-glass window and be done with it? Dropping to a squat, he started to help the person—it was a woman, he realized—gather her things. "I didn't mean to—"

Whoa.

An irritated and striking gaze—not quite gray, but not quite green, either, rimmed by a thick fan of black lashes—flicked up at him, emptying his brain of all rational thought.

"Hey!" Her husky murmur of a voice slid right under his skin, making nerve endings tighten all up and down his bare arms. "Watch where you're go…"

The end of her sentence trailed off as she got a good look at him. Her eyes widened with what he assumed was feminine appreciation.

He got that a lot. Women found him attractive, and he knew it. No big deal.

Usually, though, it didn't make him feel hot and flustered, a feeling he best remembered from sixth grade, when Yvette Connor passed him a note after English class.

He and the woman stared at each other for an electric moment.

Mid-twenties, he decided. She wasn't wearing makeup and didn't need it, not with those eyes, that smooth olive skin and that pouty berry mouth. Her hair swung in sleek black curtains, and her tank top dipped in front as she looked away and scurried to pick up her books, revealing a hint of cleavage that would be right at home in a *Playboy* centerfold.

Her scent was sweet and musky—vanilla tinged with sensual woman, two of his favorite things in the world.

His brain was slow to return, but eventually it slammed back into his body and got to work again.

"Sorry," he said. "Usually I'm much more graceful than that. The Dance Theatre keeps begging me to join, but I don't want to make the other dancers look bad." He shrugged. "You know how it is."

Lips curling, she eyed his table, where the scone waited for him. "That explains the power breakfast."

He grinned. She grinned back, and that dimpled flash of white dazzled him like a pound of diamonds glittering in the sun.

But before he lapsed into more staring, he gave himself a swift mental kick along with a reminder to get his head back in the game.

"You're not injured, are you?"

"Too soon to tell." At this point, she had all her books and there was no reason for them to remain crouched on the floor. "You could help me up."

If that meant he could touch her? Hell to the yeah. "My pleasure."

He surged to his feet and extended his hand. She took it. And as her warm palm slid across his, he felt the charge all through his body. Awareness. Electricity. Chemistry.

Focus, Hamilton.

With a gentle tug, he pulled her up and then, suddenly, they were face-to-face, with only her books between them.

Dropping her gaze and her hand, she backed away first. "Thanks."

"So." He tried not to check her out, but it was hard because he was a man and she was smokin'. About a head shorter than he was, she had the toned arms and shoulders of someone who took care of herself in the gym…khaki cargo pants…manicured toes in flat sandals…no wedding ring. There was no unobtrusive way to lean around her and check out her ass, but he wanted to and bookmarked the idea in his mind, not that there was any chance of forgetting. "Let me replace your breakfast. Least I can do."

"That would be great." She kept her gaze lowered, which really wasn't working for him, because he was getting the distinct impression she didn't want to send him any "I'm available" vibes. Was she here with someone, then? Was the lucky punk in the john washing his hands at this very second? Or had Jake mistaken the look she'd just given him? "Thanks."

"Cappuccino, right? Lots of that frothy stuff?"

She dimpled and flashed him a quick look. "That would be milk. Whole milk."

"Well, it's up to you how you ruin your coffee. And lemon cake?"

"Excuse me," Ashley the barista said sourly, edging between them with a broom, dustpan and mop. "I better clean this up."

"Thanks, Ashley," he said.

Ashley, who'd apparently undergone an attitude transplant in the past couple minutes, split her assessing gaze between the two of them before she worked on the mess. If her thinning lips were any indication, she didn't like what she saw—not the flirting or the splatter zone.

"Yeah," the woman told him. "Lemon cake."

"I'll be right back."

He hurried over to the counter and ordered, his mind full of how he and Gorgeous could eat and sip their coffee together, and then maybe grab lunch. Well, no, not lunch, obviously, right after eating breakfast, and he still needed to go home and shower because he probably smelled like the inside of his gym bag. But he'd get her number, and they could meet up later, maybe for drinks, but preferably for dinner, and then—

He swung back around, her cappuccino and cake in hand, and faltered.

She was sitting at the table in front of his, spreading out her books and opening her laptop, and didn't look like she was in the market for a session of *getting to know you* with him.

Well, shit, he thought, deflating. That wasn't the body language he'd been hoping for.

Still, there was nothing a trial lawyer liked better than a challenge, right?

He strode to her table and plunked her items in front of her. She'd put on a pair of sleek black-rimmed glasses and was all business now as she glanced up and gave him a quick nod of thanks.

"I appreciate it."

"You're welcome."

Opening a notebook, she flipped a couple pages and started tapping on her computer, dismissing him.

Okay, then. He faltered again, deflating a little more. Another minute with this one and he'd be flatter than a sheet of tracing paper.

With nothing else to do, he took a chair at his table so that they were sitting back-to-back, sipped his coffee in a moody silence and remembered, too late, that he'd forgotten his newspapers again. He could go up and get them, of course, but a third trip to the counter in three minutes would just be pathetic.

He sat. Sipped. Took a bite of scone and chewed it, tasting nothing.

Behind him, he heard relentless typing. She was working, then. Good for her. He should be working, too.

And he would leave her alone. It would be rude to disturb someone who was clearly so busy.

Screw it. He twisted at the waist and squinted at her book. "Civil procedure, eh?"

"Uh-huh," she murmured without looking up.

"That makes you a law student."

"It does indeed. Part-time."

"Where do you go?"

"Temple."

"Good school."

"It better be, because it's getting all my pennies these days."

Well, she wasn't looking at him, but she hadn't ordered him to shut the hell up, either, so he chose to believe he was making progress.

"Part-time's a rough way to go, though. It'll take you forever instead of just three years, right?"

She shrugged. "Well, you know. Full-time job and all that. Someone's got to pay for bills and tuition, so what can I do?"

He felt a wave of sympathy, because that was a backbreaking load for anyone. Yet, he felt a stronger wave of admiration, because one look at this woman's squared shoulders and firm chin told him that she was the determined type, and nothing was going to slow her down.

"What about student loans?"

"No loans for me. If I graduate with all kinds of debt, I'll have to take a job at a huge firm to pay for it. And then I won't be able to work with Legal Aid or the government if I want to. I want to keep my options open, you know?"

Another swell of appreciation hit him. "I do know. So are you enjoying it?"

"As much as anyone enjoys law school, I guess."

He cocked his head, remembering. "I enjoyed law school."

"Ah, but were you working full-time when you went?"

"I was not," he conceded. "Props to you."

Her lips turned up in the beginnings of a smile. "Why, thank you."

He sipped again. She flipped a page in her book.

He gave up on being subtle, although, to be fair, that horse had galloped out of the barn a while back when he'd first laid eyes on her.

"I notice you have…one, two, three empty chairs at your table."

That got a laugh out of her. "You didn't mention you were a math whiz."

"And I have…one, two, three empty chairs at my table. It seems like a waste of resources, don't you think?"

She heaved a long-suffering sigh, but he could hear the amusement in her voice. "You do see that I'm trying to study, right?"

"What a nice offer." Without giving her the chance to object, he gathered up his cup and plate and slid around to one of the empty chairs at her table. "I'd love to join you. I hate to eat alone. And I can help you study."

She sat back, shifting slightly to sling one of her

arms over the back of her chair, and narrowed her eyes at him. "Subtle, much?"

"What's *subtle?*"

"Wow." Her grin was wry. "That explains a lot."

"Subtlety is overrated. Everyone says so."

"Well, if you're going to help me study, here's what I need." She held up her hands and started counting on her fingers. "Number one. Read these thirty pages for me." She pointed to her red textbook which, he knew from personal experience, weighed approximately five pounds. "Number two. Summarize it for me in basic terms. None of that legal mumbo jumbo. And none of that *res ipsa* nonsense."

Oh, she was funny. "Anything else?"

"Number three. Type up my outline for me. Number four. Take the final for me. It's in December. Thanks ever so much. I'm going for a massage."

"So you want to get through your class with no reading or studying, no Latin and no exam. Does that about cover it?"

"You're the one who offered to help."

"True. I'd better keep my strength up, eh?"

His appetite restored, he took a big bite of pumpkin scone. Delicious.

Frowning down at her lemon cake, she tapped her pen on the table.

"What's wrong?"

"I think I ordered the wrong thing," she said. "What is that, anyway?"

"It's my fantastic pumpkin scone. They're out of

them, but since you're sharing your table with me, I can share this with you. Fair is fair."

"Oh, no, I—"

"I insist."

He broke the scone in half and gave her a piece. His reward? A gleeful smile that made something tighten low in his belly. Taking a bite, she made a soft sound of pleasure that rippled over his skin like warm bathwater.

"I have a new favorite," she told him.

"I knew you would."

She shoved her plate across the table at him. "You can have it. You probably need the calories after your— What exactly have you been doing to get so sweaty? I'm almost afraid to ask."

"Just a healthy workout at the gym."

"Training for the Olympics?"

"Go big or go home. That's my motto."

Sometime during this conversation, he realized suddenly, they'd adopted the same posture. Both of them had their elbows on the table and were leaning toward each other. There was an easiness about talking to her that made him feel as though he'd stumbled across a friend he hadn't seen in years, but sorely missed. It wasn't hard to imagine sitting here with her until closing time at eleven or so tonight, chatting about every little thing that might cross their minds.

A clang and a scrape startled them. It was with some surprise that he looked around and discovered that they were not, in fact, the only two people left in the Starbucks. Ashley, who'd been wiping down the table next to theirs, clanked another few pieces of silverware into her plastic bin and straightened the remaining chairs with an annoyed clunk. Lobbying a final glare at him, she took her cleaning supplies and marched through a door to the kitchen in the back.

All of this seemed to amuse his companion, who had a brow raised. "I think you've offended Ashley."

Shaking his head, he took a quick gulp of coffee. "I don't know what you're talking about."

"She's into you."

He took another sip, which was a mistake, given his overheated cheeks. "It's nothing."

She laughed and worked on another bite of scone. "If you say so. But I suggest you have your food tested for poison the next time she serves you something."

"Duly noted. So how do you manage your time with the class and work?"

She waved a hand, dismissing the topic. Apparently, this one didn't spend too much time feeling sorry for herself. "It's easy once you stop sleeping. And hobbies are out. And I don't have as much time to clean my apartment, but you won't find me crying about that."

"And what did you do for fun before you started law school?"

"Well, I spent a lot more time with my friends. I read books. Mysteries," she added, before he could ask. "And I practiced yoga."

Well, that explained the body. God bless yoga.

"Your friends understand, though, right?" he asked,

hoping she might allude to a significant other, if there was one. "They don't give you a hard time, do they?"

"They do understand. Which doesn't mean they don't whine when I miss girls' night out. But they're used to it by now."

"Good."

"And what do you do with yourself when you're not working?"

The question threw him for a major loop, probably because he was thirty-one and had no life. He hesitated, thinking of all the exciting things he wanted to do one day when he had time. When he wasn't overloaded with court appearances, needy clients and a demanding family.

Was such a magical day even possible?

Yeah, he thought sourly. *As soon as dinosaurs once again roamed the earth.*

"I'm always working," he said.

Wow. That reeked of dissatisfaction, didn't it?

She'd noticed. Her gaze sharpened with interest. "So are you a workaholic because you enjoy it or because you can't see any other way?"

Another tough question. "I have no idea."

She smiled, and her extraordinary eyes were full of understanding. "You should probably work on that, shouldn't you?"

"You're one to talk."

"Hypocrisy is my middle name."

That got him. He grinned. She grinned back. The

moment lengthened into an interlude so delicious it was almost unbearable.

He couldn't take his eyes off her.

He thought about how his day started in the usual manner—yawn worthy—and how exciting she'd made it when he least expected it. He thought about how interesting and beautiful she was, and how she'd already made him smile more this morning than he had in the past week or so, and it wasn't even noon yet.

She intrigued him more than any woman he'd met in a long time.

A *long* time.

What if he hadn't literally stumbled on to her here in Starbucks?

What if his attraction was one-sided?

He didn't think so, though. Her eyes were too bright and her color too high.

And he'd been around long enough to know when a woman responded to him.

She turned away first, running an unsteady hand through her hair. "Well…"

He cleared his throat, which felt tight with a sudden longing that was all out of proportion with the occasion. Sharing coffee and a breakfast treat with a complete stranger shouldn't tie him up in knots, he knew, no matter how sexy she was.

Tell that to his raging hormones.

"Well," he said.

With her head bent low, she flipped a couple pages forward in her book, and then flipped back again. Ultimately, she pushed away the book and pulled the laptop closer, tapping a couple keys. He had the idea she was as flustered as he was, which made him feel a whole lot better, because he was a sudden mass of nerves, desire and uncertainty.

"I should get back to studying." She tipped up her face just enough for him to see deepening frown lines between her brows. "I don't mean to be rude, but I have a lot of work to do and not a lot of time to do it."

Ah, man. Was he a jerk, or what? He rolled his shoulders, trying to release some of his spiking tension. "Sorry. I'm saying that to you a lot, aren't I?"

"It's okay," she said quickly. "It was fun talking to you. But the being-knocked-on-my-butt part? Not so fun."

He snorted out a laugh.

"But I liked the scone. Thanks for introducing me to something new."

He slid back his chair with a loud scrape that echoed his frustration. "I'll just…go on back to my own table and leave you in peace."

"Give a yell if you get lost."

The teasing undid him. He wanted more of it. More of her.

The words came out in a rush. "Have dinner with me tonight."

Her head came up, and she hit him with that intense gaze and eyes that were round and shocked. "Excuse me?"

His hopes crashed and burned via a sickening swoop

in his belly. "I knew it. You're with someone, aren't you?"

"What? No, but I just don't think it's a good idea. Do you?"

"Dinner is always a good idea. You have food, maybe some wine, you get nourishment—it's great."

"Don't you think both our lives are complicated enough without rocking the boat?"

"I thrive on complications."

"I don't, though," she said flatly. "I thrive on smooth sailing."

Jake took a minute to regroup, thinking hard. He'd asked her out, she'd said no, end of story. He wasn't in the habit of begging women to be with him, and his pride wouldn't let him start now. She wasn't the only woman in Philly, and if she wasn't interested in him, well, then screw her. Her loss.

So why did *he* feel like the biggest loser? Why did he have the uncomfortable certainty that something special was slipping through his fingers?

He stared at her, trying to manage his disappointment. "How can I change your mind? I'm just talking dinner here. You have my permission to walk out on me if you're not having fun. You can duck into the ladies' room and never come back."

For a minute, she wavered, dimpling, and he thought he had her.

But then her expression hardened and she shook her head. "I'm not going out with you. You shouldn't even be asking me." She gave him a little wave. "Buh-bye."

Shouldn't even be asking?

Okay. Why was he getting the feeling he was missing something?

"Why shouldn't I be ask—"

"Wow," said a new voice. A mocking female voice, to be exact. "Some things never change, do they? I should have known."

Hang on. He knew that voice. Jake looked up and— Aah, shit.

Speaking of unneeded complications.

"Avery." He kept his expression cool. "What're you doing here?"

Avery, a pretty brunette he'd met at the gym and with whom he'd shared a couple—no, three—memorable interludes at her place, loomed over the table. Apparently she'd also just come from working out, because she had a duffel slung over her shoulder and was wearing shorts and a sports top.

She looked pissed. Her eyes were narrowed, her lips were thin and one manicured hand was firmly planted on a hip. The killing glare she leveled on him warned that she'd be overturning tables and kicking asses in a minute.

His gorgeous companion, meanwhile, had a single brow raised and was watching for his reaction.

"I stopped in for some juice," Avery said. "But while I'm here, maybe you could explain why you haven't been returning my texts. Is *she* the reason? What am I saying? Of course she is."

A couple nearby heads swiveled in their direction,

probably because Avery's volume was on the increase. As always, when someone was upset, he kept his tone low and reasonable.

"Avery, I told you I wouldn't be seeing you anymore," he reminded her.

"No, jackass. What you said was that you were busy at work and would call me in a few days. That was three weeks ago."

His conscience squirmed guiltily. That *did* sound like something he'd say.

He opened his mouth with no real idea of how he could smooth things over.

Avery saved him the trouble by dumping her cup of juice in his lap.

Iced juice.

Yelping, he leaped to his feet, dimly aware of the gasps and snickers all around him. Ashley the barista, in particular, gave a loud snort, which he did not appreciate.

Ah, but Avery wasn't done with him yet.

"Great glasses," Avery said to Gorgeous. "Dolce & Gabbana?"

Gorgeous, looking startled, touched her frames. "Uh, yes. Thanks."

"You're welcome." Avery hitched her bag higher on her shoulder and gave the woman a rueful smile. "Let me give you a piece of advice, girlfriend. This one?" She jabbed a finger in Jake's direction; he winced. "He's good for about three orgasms for about three nights."

"Avery," he growled.

"So enjoy it while it lasts," Avery continued. "But don't get your feelings involved. Okay? Gotta go, people. Bye."

Avery wheeled around and swept through the glass door—thank the Good Lord—but the damage was done. Not that he'd been on firm footing with Gorgeous anyway.

Looking grim, she was gathering up her books and laptop and cramming them back into her bag with jerky movements. "I'm leaving, too."

Fully aware of how ridiculous he looked with the juice stain down his crotch, he tried to do some major damage control. If she walked out of here now, he was certain both that he'd never see her again and that her memory would haunt him for a good long time.

"That's never happened to me before," he said quickly.

"Right," she said, yanking her bag's zipper closed. "Whatever you say."

"I know that looked bad," he continued, lowering his voice because he was anxious not to give the avid onlookers anything else to laugh about, "but we never had a, uh, real relationship. We just, uh, hooked up."

"It's none of my business."

She turned to go. He gave it one last shot. That was his nature. He fought for the important things in life. And he knew, on some instinctual and inexplicable level, that she was important.

"Wait," he called after her, not caring who was listening. What was a little more humiliation on top of what he'd already endured? "At least tell me your name."

She swung back around and gaped at him with more horror than he thought was necessary under the circumstances. "Oh, my God. You have no idea who I am, do you?"

Uh-oh. That didn't sound good.

He froze, thinking hard and fast.

Had they met before? And, if so, how could he ever have forgotten her?

"No," he admitted. "Who are you?"

Her eyes, which were now a definite and stormy gray, flashed so much ice at him that he felt his veins constrict with the cold.

"Someone you'll never be *hooking up* with, buddy. You can count on that."

Chapter 2

This. Could. Not. Be. Happening.

Charlotte Evans tried to regulate her panicked breathing the following Monday morning, which wasn't easy while sprinting up the back staircase of Hamilton, Hamilton and Clark. In a pencil skirt and heels.

She should be sitting at her cubicle on the lower level—affectionately known as The Dungeon—of the law firm's redbrick building, with all the other typing pool peons. She should be keeping her head down and tapping out ninety words per minute so that the work in her inbox didn't continue to multiply until it smothered her.

Now was no time for a personal crisis.

The appellate brief she was currently working on

needed to be filed with the Third Circuit by noon. N-O-O-N. Which was—she checked her watch—less than three hours from now. Three short hours! How in God's name was she going to decipher all the microscopic red edits by then? And how was she going to finish—

Later for that alarming thought. Reaching the firm's reception area, which was on the fourth floor, she took a deep breath, smoothed her skirt and crept through the heavy fire door.

As usual, the stately leather and mahogany made her feel like a clumsy little kid again, as though her mother would show up and smack away her hands if she touched anything too expensive or precious. Which was pretty much anything in the reception area, where clients had their first impression of the firm. There were oversize windows framed by striped silk drapes, potted palms in every corner, Oriental lamps and rugs that probably cost more than her beat-up used car was worth, and a crystal chandelier that sparkled like flawless diamonds against the carved ceiling moldings.

Meredith, the receptionist, gatekeeper and queen of all she surveyed up here, sat at her post behind the granite counter. Her headset was in place and her phone-answering voice was singsong perfect.

"Good morning. Thank you for calling Hamilton, Hamilton and Clark," she was murmuring into her mic. "How may I direct your call?"

The only thing out of place on this floor that showcased the extreme elegance of one of Philadelphia's most prestigious law firms, Charlotte thought, was—

"Mommy!"

Right over there. The two-year-old boy taking the M&M's out of the Waterford crystal candy jar on the nearest coffee table and alternately eating them and hiding them in the dried moss in one of the palm's pots.

Wonderful.

"Hi, cutie." Grinning and stooping, she caught Harry, her shrieking son, as he sprinted across the seating area. "Shhh," she told him, even though she knew it was a useless exercise, because Harry only had one volume, which was loud, and one speed, which was fast. "We use our quiet voice and walking feet at Mommy's work, okay?"

"I am using my quiet voice!" Harry informed her, his gray eyes wide and affronted.

Ignoring the disapproving glance from Meredith, who was still talking into her headset and pushing buttons on her phone, Charlotte settled Harry on her hip and gave him a discreet mother's once-over.

The first thing she noticed, due to the telltale area of flattened black curls in the back, was that his hair hadn't been combed. So that was a demerit right there. On the plus side, he'd brushed his teeth. On the minus side, though, he was sporting dried toothpaste on the corner of his mouth. Oh, and a swath of what looked like dried syrup on one chipmunk cheek. Nice.

Continuing on to the clothes front, there was bad news: he was wearing his Bugs Bunny pajamas. With the feet. Which might explain why his Velcro gym shoes were on the wrong feet, but, then again, might not.

The bottom line? Her adorable and generally clean son had returned from a night with his father looking like a refugee.

Typical.

Still, this two-year-old ragamuffin was the love of her life, and she was glad to see him, even if this was a very bad time. Nuzzling his chubby little face, she turned to his father, whom she was not glad to see.

Roger Miller stood there in blue scrubs and athletic shoes, furiously thumbing buttons on his smartphone.

Also typical.

For the last year of their relationship, which had ended about a year ago, the only parts of Roger she'd seen were the top of his head as he texted and answered emails, and the back of him, as he left to go back to the hospital, which was the love of *his* life.

She was not in the mood for waiting for the oh-so-important surgical resident to acknowledge her, but she hid her irritation behind a pleasant voice for Harry's sake.

"What's going on, Roger? You know I'm working."

Lowering the phone, he glanced up at her with those brown eyes and managed to look moderately rueful. "I know, but I'm on call, and they called me. I have to get to the hospital in half an hour and scrub in. There's nothing I can do about it."

"But, Roger," she said, as sweetly as she could with her spiking temper, "I'm also working. As you can see."

He waved a hand. "Why can't you get one of the other secretaries to cover for you until you can take him to day care after lunch? How big a deal could that be?"

Okay. Forget sweet.

"A very big deal."

They glared at each other across the top of Harry's head, and then Meredith intervened.

"I'm going to the kitchen for a snack," she called over the counter. "Does anyone out there want a cookie?"

"Me!" Vaulting out of Charlotte's arms like an Olympic gymnast in training, Harry ran across the reception area on his tiny little mismatched feet and took Meredith's hand when she offered it to him. "And I want a double cappuccino iced tea, too!"

Meredith's laughter disappeared down the long hallway to the kitchen. "I'll see what I can do."

"Thanks, Meredith," Charlotte called.

Meredith waved.

Charlotte turned back to Roger and took a long minute to wrestle her temper under control. They were a team, and she needed to remember that. A united team with a single crucial goal: to raise Harry into a happy and contributing member of society. As a team, they needed to negotiate and compromise, and as a mother, she needed to not throttle her baby daddy.

No matter how hard said baby daddy made it on her at times.

"I can't take him right now, Roger."

A look of absolute befuddlement crossed over Roger's features, giving Charlotte the feeling that she'd really challenged his imagination by suggesting that anything about her lowly job could matter to anyone.

There went her self-esteem, slipping another several notches.

As though Jake Hamilton hadn't done enough of a job on it the other day by not remembering her from work. The whole time they were chatting it up at Starbucks, he'd had no idea that she was one of his employees.

None.

True, they worked on separate floors and had only interacted, in passing, at the firm's occasional staff appreciation luncheons. He wasn't involved in the firm's hiring process and had probably never had the need to come to the catacombs, where she worked. True, she hadn't laid eyes on him in several months, probably since the last staff Christmas party, and then only from a distance across the crowded conference room.

But, still.

How could she feel good about herself when she'd made such a non-impression on him? When she recognized not only him, but all the other Hamiltons who worked at the firm, because she made it her business to know the faces of the people who put food on her table? The bottom line was that she'd been here at the firm for years and he didn't recognize her or know that he and his family were her employers.

He did not, in short, know her from Adam or Eve.

Yeah. That had been a swift kick to the solar plexus. Especially because she was so exquisitely aware of who *he* was and had been since the second she first laid eyes on him. She'd been a brand-new employee the day that he strode out of the elevator and gave her a crisp nod as she was getting on.

She'd been stunned.

What woman wouldn't be?

And now, two days after their interlude at Starbucks, she was still deflated and agitated, her poor stupid head filled with images of the unexpected heat she'd seen in Jake's eyes, and Jake probably hadn't given her a second thought. He'd probably hooked up with Ashley the barista, Avery the disgruntled sex buddy, or any one of the dozens of women he probably kept dangling at any given time.

The jerk.

A sexy jerk, yeah, but still a jerk.

Anyway, the issue now wasn't Jake Hamilton, or how much he'd seemed *into her* the other day, or how he'd asked her out to dinner, or how he was, in fact, nothing but an inveterate player who'd probably only hit on her at Starbucks because it was a reflex with him, like coughing when his throat was dry.

The issue was her self-esteem, which had been in a steady decline for ages, ever since she told Roger about her accidental pregnancy (ripped condom) and saw the look of absolute horror on his face. It was as though the only thing worse than having an unplanned baby at that point in his life was having an unplanned baby with *her*.

Then there'd been the breakup, which wasn't quite as brutal as the one in that old movie *The War of the Roses* but had been tough nonetheless. Then they'd gone to court to establish everyone's parental responsibilities, and then she'd shelved her plans to go to law school full-time because she had to also work and support a child.

Roger, meanwhile, had blithely continued with his education and career because his daddy had more money than God and was happy to foot the bill.

Must be nice, eh?

Now she was a typing drone in the secretarial pool, a single mother juggling diapers, toddler tantrums, unscheduled illnesses and pediatric visits, and a part-time law student managing a class a semester. He, on the other hand, was deep into his residency and well on his way to becoming a real-life Dr. McDreamy.

Not that she was bitter, she thought, crossing her arms over her chest and glaring at him. Much.

But at the rate she was going, he'd be a millionaire with a thriving practice and his first yacht while she was still trying to finish a first-year law student's course load.

Was it any wonder she felt invisible half the time?

Well, she was sick of it. Sick of being a second-class citizen—and an invisible one, at that. If she didn't stand up for herself and her needs, who would? Roger? Please.

She was tired of being a doormat, and it was going to stop.

Right now.

Roger seemed to have given up on trying to understand how her job was relevant, and moved on to the only important thing in any conversation, as far as he

was concerned: his wants and needs and any petty an-
noyances that might inconvenience him.

"Why can't you call your mother to come pick Harry
up?" he asked, a note of challenge in his voice now.

"Well, first of all, since today is your day with Harry,
it's your responsibility to care for him. Not mine," she
reminded him. He scowled. "Second, even if I wanted
to call her, my mother is in doctor's appointments and
physical therapy for most of the day."

"Shit," Roger muttered, mostly to himself. "What
am I going to do now?"

His narcissism was really amazing, she thought. True
and pure, as unadulterated as winter's first snow.

"Mom's doing pretty well, by the way. Thanks for
asking. She has much more energy after the heart procedure."

Roger's lips thinned with growing annoyance. "Glad
to hear it. I always liked her."

"Right." She checked her watch and saw how much
of her precious time had ticked away. That brief wasn't
going to type itself. Not to mention the fact that this was
the floor Jake Hamilton worked on, and the longer she
hung out here, the greater her chances of running into
him, which would be awkward, to say the least. So she
and Roger needed to wrap this up so she could go back
to the basement, where she belonged.

"You need to take Harry and go, okay? Drop him
off at *your* mother's or something. She's always glad
to see—"

"I can't," Roger said flatly. "I don't want to interrupt her spa day. You'll have to—"

Sentences that began with *you'll have to* always ended badly. It was a rule.

Accordingly, she marched up to Roger and got in his face. So much for being a team.

"Kindly do not tell me what I need to do," she began, keeping her voice low, because he would not reduce her to a banshee here at her place of employment. Thank God there was no one else around at the moment to see this developing scene; the last thing she needed was gossip. She always took great pains to keep her private life *private,* and the other staff would have a field day with any little tidbit about her personal life. "You need to call in to the hospital and tell them that—"

Roger loomed over her, his features contorted with anger. "I can't just—"

"Is there a problem?" asked a cool male voice behind her.

Oh, God.

Charlotte stiffened with sudden paralysis, and the bottom dropped out of her stomach like a stone, probably landing somewhere deep in Philly's sewer system.

She knew that voice. That voice belonged to the absolute last person she wanted to see. That voice, like the person who owned it, was nothing but trouble.

Roger's arrogant gaze flickered past her shoulder, and his voice, when he spoke, was so condescending that she wanted to dropkick him into next year.

"I don't believe anyone asked for your input, my brother."

Apparently Jake Hamilton felt the same way about harming Roger. His frigid tone, when he responded, was like being assaulted with ice chards.

"I'm afraid you're getting my input, *my brother*. Since you're standing in my building and badgering a woman, you'll be getting *a lot* of my input."

Roger's face turned a blotchy and angry purple.

Uh-oh.

"It's okay," Charlotte said quickly, trying to defuse the situation before these two badasses decided to take their dispute outside or something. Embracing her inner coward, she kept her back to Jake and hoped he didn't recognize her voice. "We were just having a—"

That was as far as she got before Jake swooped in, clamped a hand on her upper arm and spun her to face him. She spluttered a protest; he ignored it. His intent gaze locked in on her face, skating over all her features as though he needed to double- and triple-check to make sure it was really her, and his emotions were raw and as readable as a Times Square billboard.

Surprise. Excitement. Wide-eyed delight.

"It's you," he said.

"Yes," she admitted, trying to calm her racing pulse.

Charlotte knew better than to let this man under her skin. Well, farther under her skin, anyway. She knew he wasn't for her under any circumstances. He was one of her bosses, for one. He was a womanizer, for another. Most importantly, she had a child to raise, a mother with dicey health to care for, a law degree to finish and no time for nonsense.

A fling with a man who, from all appearances, flirted with anything with boobs, definitely qualified as nonsense.

Duh.

And yet, as she stared into the vivid brown flash of his eyes and saw the color rise over his cheekbones, it was hard to remember any of her concerns.

Jake Hamilton was breathtaking.

On Saturday, he'd been boyish and accessible, his loose-limbed body tall, muscular and athletic in those knit shorts and shirt. She'd been arrested by the span of his shoulders, the sinew of his arms and legs and the unmistakable roundness of his butt.

Today he was all dark-suited, red-tied business. His shirt was starched, his cuff links were shiny, and his shoes were buffed to the kind of polish that required sunglasses to protect the eyes.

And his face—

Intelligent brown eyes framed by heavy brows. Angular cheekbones. Full lips that probably spent an inordinate amount of time kissing one woman or another. Skin so smooth she longed to run her hands all over it—every inch—just to see if she could find a flaw.

When he looked at her, she felt hot.

When she looked at him, she felt breathless.

Not a good combination if she wanted to keep her head, was it?

When you looked like Jake Hamilton, she wondered,

was it really your fault that women trailed you the way rats trailed the Pied Piper?

No, she decided.

But that didn't mean she had to be a rat.

"What's your name?" Jake demanded.

"Charlotte Evans."

"What are you doing here?"

Thanks for the reminder, Jake.

He *still* had no clue that they'd been working in the same building for years. She *still* meant nothing to him. Never had, never would.

"I work here," she said flatly.

Those brows lowered, creating a thundercloud effect that would have been pretty funny under any other circumstances. He cocked his ear, probably to make sure it wasn't playing tricks on him.

"You—" he began, faltering.

"Work here, yes," she finished for him. "For two years now. In the secretarial pool. Thanks for remembering."

"Now that the introductions are finished," interjected Roger, "I'd appreciate it if I could finish up my conversation with Charlotte, okay? Thanks."

Jake stilled, except for the tightening of his jaw, and focused all his fierce energy on Roger.

Roger blinked, looking away first with a huff of impatience.

"And you are?" Jake asked in a tone appropriate for asking a dog why he was pooping on his freshly shampooed carpet.

"Roger Miller."

They did not shake hands, which was probably for the best. There was so much negativity in the air at the moment that any physical contact between the two men would probably lead to an arm-wrestling contest followed by the snapping of someone's arm as it broke in two.

"And why are you here, Roger?" Jake's voice was silky smoothness over a layer of unyielding granite. "Interrupting my employee's workday and upsetting her?"

Roger's lips thinned. He opened his mouth to say something that would probably be pissy if not outright rude, but there was a new interruption.

Small footsteps raced up the hallway from the kitchen, and Harry, now holding a to-go coffee cup that thankfully had a lid on it, ran into view. *Please, God,* she prayed, *do NOT let this child drop his drink on this expensive rug.*

"Look, Mommy!" In his typical greeting, Harry launched himself at her legs, giving her a quick, one-handed hug before holding up his arms and demanding to be lifted. She obliged, settling him on her hip. "I have a chocolate milk-a-ccino. Taste it!"

He offered the cup, which was smeared with something that may once have been chocolate but was now disgusting.

She tried to look rueful as she declined this generous offer. "Maybe in a minute, Harry."

Harry, luckily, rarely stayed on one subject long

enough to get his feelings hurt. "Who's that?" He pointed a fat and smudgy finger at Jake.

"That's my boss, Mr. Hamilton," she told Harry. "I work for him."

Harry gave Jake an appraising look. "I'm Harry. I'm four." He held up four fingers.

"Nice try." Charlotte adjusted his fingers down to two. "You know how old you are. Stop trying to pretend you're older."

Harry scowled at her for calling him out, and then sipped his milk in what he apparently thought was a dignified manner.

The weight of Jake's gaze felt as though someone had covered her face with a lead blanket. Deciding that she'd avoided the moment long enough, she hitched up her chin and looked at him over Harry's head, feeling defiant.

His reaction to this news that she was a single mother—he'd figure out that she and Roger had never been married soon enough—didn't matter to her. Of course it didn't. If people judged her harshly, then that was their problem, not hers. She loved Harry, who was the pride of her life, and anyone who thought less of her personal situation was a moron. And her life was too full and busy to waste time with morons.

It was just that she'd had a few painful and best-forgotten experiences with men who had wanted to date her, found out she had a kid, then took the next train to *I'm outta here,* never to be seen again.

Jake's expression was still. Dark. Utterly unreadable.

They stared at each other for one lengthy and terrible moment before Jake broke free of whatever had him in its grip. Something about him eased up, making him much less forbidding, and he studied Harry for a second or two.

Harry, all wide-eyed and fat-cheeked behind his cup, stared back.

"So you're two, eh?" Jake's lips curled into a half smile. "That makes you old enough to get a job, doesn't it, little dude?"

Harry darted Charlotte an incredulous glance and squealed with laughter. "A job? No way!"

"Well, you're welcome to hang out at the office for as long as you need to, anyway. Kids are always welcome here," Jake informed him.

Charlotte's jaw dropped.

"We'll find something for you to do, okay?" Jake continued. "God knows some of the lawyers around here aren't that much smarter than you. How does that sound?"

Harry grinned, revealing his tiny set of perfectly white teeth. "Great. Yay!"

With a definitive nod, Jake adjusted his cuffs and spared Roger a sidelong look that was none too warm. "I'll let you two wrap things up." He paused. "Quickly."

"Thanks," Charlotte said.

Jake leveled all of his attention on her, which gave

her the uncomfortable sensation of being a butterfly pinned to someone's board.

"I'll need to see you in my office," he said as he strode off. "Five minutes."

Chapter 3

Jake planted his palms on his desk and leaned into it, struggling to master his thoughts. His thoughts did not want to be mastered. They were, in fact, spinning out of control, as though his head had become a child's top, ricocheting off walls and furniture legs with no sign of stopping.

After a weekend of high agitation, no sleep and stalking the Starbucks for any sign of her, he'd found his mystery woman.

Well, *found* wasn't exactly the right word, was it?

He'd stumbled on to his mystery woman.

He'd discovered that his mystery woman was no real mystery, after all.

She'd been working right here, in this very building,

under his very nose, for the past couple years, and he was willing to swear on a stack of Bibles that he'd never seen her before in his life, because how could he have ever laid eyes on a woman like that and forgotten her?

He must have, though.

Which made him a dumbass.

A blind dumbass, to be precise, and that was not a good feeling.

Shit.

Sudden exhaustion made him slump into his leather chair.

Renewed agitation made him get back up again and pace.

Charlotte Evans. A firm employee. And since he was a partner in the firm, that made her *his* employee.

A man couldn't go around lusting after his employees, not unless he wanted to get sued for sexual harassment. And if he did enter into a discreet, consensual relationship with Charlotte—a big *if,* considering he didn't know the status of her relationship with *Dr. Punko* out there—word would get out. Word always got out. And what would happen then? Office morale would plummet, for one. And his family would hand him his head on a platter for introducing his personal drama into the workplace, for another.

Double *shit.*

So where did that leave him?

Screwed, that's where.

Because he thought about Charlotte Evans, firm employee. He saw her eyes when he didn't want to. Heard her laugh when he wanted silence. Had been haunted by her all weekend.

Wanted her.

After about the tenth lap of his office, he wore himself out and rested a hip on the edge of his desk. And what about—

There was a soft knock on his ajar door, and Charlotte poked her head inside. "Hi."

Snapping to attention with an abrupt spike in his pulse rate, he stood. "Come in."

"Come on, little man." Tugging Harry's hand, she ushered him inside the office and tried to steer him toward the tufted leather sofa against the far wall. "I want you to sit right here and be very—"

But Harry had seen the large jar of M&M's on Jake's desk.

"Candy, Mommy!"

"Not a chance," she told him.

No worries. Harry wheeled around, spotted the giant aquarium of tropical fish and plants and veered in that direction with a shout of surprised delight that made Jake grin. "Look, Mommy! Fish!" Harry raced over and pointed at the orange one with black and white stripes. "And look! There's Nemo! Hi, Nemo!"

Charlotte shot Jake an apologetic look. "Harry ends every sentence with an exclamation point, in case you hadn't noticed. Don't tap on the glass, Harry. It disturbs the fish, okay?" It didn't seem to matter, though, because Harry now had both palms and his nose pressed up against the aquarium and was in toddler rapture, murmuring to the fish. "Sorry about the fingerprints," she told Jake, lowering her voice. "And I told Roger that I couldn't have Harry here, but—"

Jake raised a hand, stopping her. "It's okay. Kids are welcome here."

"That's very nice of you, but it's a law firm, and Harry has no idea what an inside voice is. Oh, and he left a half pound of M&M's in the potted plant in the reception area, and his typing sucks."

Jake laughed.

"So I need to get him out of here. And I will. I just need to—"

"I didn't know you had a child."

Jake resisted the urge to clap his hand over his big mouth. Whoa. Where had that come from? And why had he said it, even if he was thinking it? He did, thankfully, restrain the follow-up question on the tip of his tongue, which had to do with Harry's father—who was clearly a punk ass if ever he'd seen one—and whether he and Charlotte had an ongoing romantic relationship.

None of his business, he knew, even if the curiosity was gnawing on his guts with sharp little teeth.

Those striking eyes of hers turned flinty. "Among other things you didn't know about me, yes." She seemed to regret her words immediately, because she fidgeted on her feet, checked her watch and then shot a quick glance at Harry to make sure he was staying out of trouble. "Look, I don't mean to be rude, but I have a brief to finish typing and it's got to be filed by noon, so I really need to—"

"Yeah. About that." Jake waved a hand at her employment file, which he'd grabbed from their HR person and flipped through in the past few minutes. "I didn't know you graduated from Penn with a degree in international relations. Which makes you uniquely overqualified for the typing pool here at the office."

A subtle flair of panic crossed over her features but, to her credit, she quickly mastered it. "Yes, but I need the full-time work and the benefits are good. I have a mouth to feed. I need a job. I need *this* job."

Admiration tugged at his mouth, making him want to smile, but he stifled it because he didn't think she'd appreciate it. "You don't get it. Keeping you in the typing pool isn't making the best use of your talents, which is foolish. And I may be blind, but I'm not foolish."

She gave him a narrow-eyed stare of suspicion. "You'll have to help me out here. What does that mean?"

"It means that I'm making you my new paralegal, effective immediately. Thereby sparing myself the time and trouble of interviewing more people. I've been pretty unimpressed with the candidates I've seen so far, and it's been a month since my old paralegal relocated to Boston."

Charlotte blinked at him, working hard to get her jaw up off the floor. "But—"

"Which means that you get the office next to mine, which has a TV in it for viewing video depositions, but you can use it to let Harry watch kid shows while he's here."

Charlotte rubbed her temple and took a moment to get her thoughts together.

"But—" she repeated weakly.

"Mommy!" Harry jumped up and down, pointing into the tank. "It's a starfish! A STARFISH, Mommy!"

"Wow. I see it," she answered before turning back to Jake. "What's going on? I don't understand this at all."

Yeah. There was a lot of that going around, apparently, because Jake didn't understand his attraction to this woman at all, or his strange compulsion to help her out where he could and make her complicated life a little bit easier. Oh, and he also didn't understand how he thought he'd work closely with her without falling deeper into lust, but he figured he'd tackle that hurdle one day at a time.

"All you need to understand is that I'm giving you a promotion to a job that's much more educational for a law student. Which comes with a fifty percent raise, by the way. But if you think you'll miss the tedium of typing for eight or nine hours every day, then feel free to refuse, and I'll continue my search for a good paralegal. It's entirely up to you."

She hesitated.

"Mommy? Mommy! Can we get a fish tank for my bedroom?"

Charlotte rolled her eyes, but Jake wanted to share a high five with the little guy for helping him make his case. Kids were expensive, weren't they? They needed and wanted things, like food, shoes and fish. A paralegal could afford many more kid things than a secretary could, and Charlotte was more than smart enough to know it.

And if dangling this tempting offer in front of a mother's nose made Jake a bit of a devil, well, that was a charge he could live with. To get to know her better he could live with it, no problem.

And the fact that he was lusting after a woman who was a mother? Also no problem, he discovered to his own surprise.

However, the fact that he was simultaneously thinking about how he could get closer to Charlotte while issuing himself stern warnings about staying the hell away from her...well, that was a problem.

A big freaking problem.

An even bigger problem was that, the longer he stared at her, the less he cared about problems, big or otherwise.

She was severe today, with her glorious hair scraped back into a bun at the nape of her neck that should be forever consigned to grannies and librarians. Plus, she was buttoned down into a navy blue suit that was so drab it made Jake want to find the designer and bludgeon him.

Even so, there was no hiding the curve of her hips or the hint of cleavage up top. Her long and sexy legs ended in a pair of pointy nude heels, the kind that were a gift to men everywhere, and her ass, in that straight skirt, was nothing short of spectacular.

Her face was tight, her lips thin and her eyes stormy as she struggled with her dilemma. And right there, served up on a silver platter for him, was the answer to one of the questions that had plagued him all weekend.

The prickling electricity he'd felt between them? She felt it, too, and she knew it could very well lead to something complicated…but interesting.

Why else would she hesitate to accept such a great promotion?

Maybe the gentlemanly thing to do would be to give her the promotion as some other attorney's paralegal. He could snap his fingers, and it would be done.

Too bad he wasn't feeling gentlemanly.

He was feeling hot and bothered, and he suspected he'd feel that way for a while. Why? Because the only cure he could imagine was unbuttoning all that armor she wore and getting inside her. And, much as he wanted to do just that, he was still rational enough to know it was a bad idea.

But he was feeling pretty irrational, too. "Ticktock," he murmured, tapping his watch.

The storm behind her eyes had turned to a glare, and her chest was heaving up and down, which was quite the sight to see, even if her ugly jacket blocked the view. She stepped closer, ready to go toe-to-toe with him, even if he was her boss.

He liked that.

"And what's in it for you?" she demanded, low.

He shrugged. "A good paralegal, I hope," he said, keeping his tone silky. "What else?"

"You hit on me the other day. Back when you had no idea who I was. I know it doesn't mean anything, because you probably hit on every woman who stands still long enough for you to ask her what her sign is—"

He scowled. For one, this assessment of his, uh, exuberant dating life cut a little too close to the bone, frankly, and, for another, his fascination with her bore no resemblance to the passing lust he felt for pretty women in general, which disturbed him.

"—but I'm not trying to be the victim of any sexual harassment. So, like I said Saturday, I don't think our spending time together is a good idea."

"I'm a professional, Charlotte. Have I done or said anything inappropriate this morning?"

"No, but—"

"You think I want to ruin my career with sexual harassment allegations?"

"Well, no, but—"

"Or maybe you think I'm so taken with you that I can't think straight or tell right from wrong."

Her defiant gaze wavered and fell. "Of course not."

Ironic, eh? His thinking didn't feel straight at all right now. Good thing she had no idea how his hands twitched for the feel of her.

And he was nothing if not a ruthless negotiator. Striding around his desk, he sank into his chair and turned to his computer, tapping a few random keys like he wanted to check his email or some such.

"Well? Yes or no? I don't have all day."

"Harry," she said sharply. "Get down from that ottoman and push it back where it was. You can't touch the fish, okay?"

Harry grumbled a response.

Jake spun his chair to face her again and stretched his arms high overhead, as though he didn't have a care in the world. Victory was close enough that he could almost stick out his tongue and taste its sweetness.

His gaze locked with Charlotte's and, honest to God, he felt magnetized, as though the pull of her could drag him across his desk and into her arms.

"What about my brief that's due this morning?" she asked.

Yes.

Triumph swelled inside him, threatening to blow him up like a kid's balloon.

"I thought I mentioned that. Another secretary is already handling it for you."

Her lips twisted into a wry smile. "You work fast, don't you?"

He stared at her, unsmiling. "The key is knowing when to work fast and when to take your time. Don't you agree?"

A flush ran up her face, making her eyes bright and her cheeks pink.

"I'm not sure this is a good idea."

Yeah. Neither was he.

"We're about to find out, aren't we, Charlotte?"

"I guess we are."

She turned to walk out, presenting him with her profile, and a chunk of memory hit him. A glimpse of that same profile leaning over the buffet table at some firm party or other. And another memory of that same profile disappearing down the hall, into the kitchen, one day as he was coming out of his office for a bathroom break.

Had he never seen this beautiful face full-on before? Was that it?

Or was it that he'd never taken the time to look?

"Charlotte," he called.

She'd just reached Harry at the aquarium, but now she paused, looking over her shoulder at him. "Yes?"

"I'm sorry."

"For what?"

Yeah, genius, for what? How did you plan to put it into words?

He paused, trying to get it right. "For never taking the time to see you."

She quickly looked away, ducking her head. "It doesn't matter."

"Yes, it does," he told her. "It matters a lot."

Charlotte sank into the tall leather chair behind the desk in her new office and tried to wrap her brain around the reversal of fortune she'd just undergone. It was impossible. If a genie had swooped out of her morning cup of coffee and granted her three wishes, she couldn't have been more surprised.

Jake Hamilton, fairy godfather.

Who'd've thought?

Adjusting the height of her chair, she eyeballed her son, who was curled into a little nest on the sofa, fast asleep. Thank goodness they still traveled with a diaper bag (the potty training had, thus far, been a resounding failure) and therefore had his blankie and a padded cushion with them at all times. And while she was saying her thanks, she also needed to give a shout-out that the boy was still young enough to need a late-morning nap and had collapsed into an exhausted heap.

Now she had a narrow window of opportunity to get some work done.

Or to reflect a little bit more on her new and improved work situation.

The raise was a dream come true. With more money coming in, she wouldn't have to agonize about whether she could afford a new humidifier for Jake's room, or a big boy twin bed so she could get him out of the crib, which he was fast outgrowing.

She could also give Mama a bit more money every month to help with her exorbitant prescription expenses. And if Charlotte saved for several months or so, she'd have enough for a new car. Well, not a *new* car, obviously, but a used car that wasn't quite as close to death as the one she had now.

Maybe she could even afford to take another class each semester and thereby manage to graduate from law school while she was still young enough to be able to remember why she wanted to be a lawyer in the first place.

The increased money was a thrill, no doubt.

So was the prospect of being able to spend her days doing something other than typing until her fingers cramped and her eyes crossed.

Leaving The Dungeon was a huge bonus, as well.

Now she might be able to catch the occasional glimpse of sunshine out her window because, yes, she had a window. And a spectacular view of Rittenhouse Square, with its bright green grass, reflecting pool and benches. Swiveling in her chair, she looked again, taking another second to enjoy the sky's vivid blue and the sight of several kids racing around there, laughing and climbing the lion and goat statues. The thrill of having something so lovely to look at couldn't have been greater if Jake had presented her with an original Picasso for her wall.

But the office itself…that was a problem.

It wasn't a paralegal's office. Not by a long shot.

This was a lawyer's office, and a nice one, at that.

Jake's corner office next door was nicer, true, but her office was large, filled with expensive and elegant leather and mahogany furniture, lush green plants, a TV and DVD player, and beautiful framed photograph prints on the walls. And, of course, there was the view.

When the other secretaries got wind of this five-star treatment, she suspected they would not be happy. Not at all.

She'd worry about that later, though. For now, she needed to—

Her desk phone beeped, and then the receptionist's voice came over the speaker. "Charlotte? I've got Jake's mother on line one. She sounds upset, so brace yourself."

Wait, *what?* "Hang on. Am I supposed to take Jake's calls?"

"Not normally, but his secretary went to the dentist and Jake didn't answer my page, so I'm putting her through to you. Good luck."

With that dire send-off, the receptionist hung up.

Charlotte studied the receiver for a second, half afraid that it would strike like a rabid dog if she got too close, took a deep breath and answered.

"Hi, Mrs. Hamilton. I'm Charlotte Evans, Jake's new paralegal. Can I help you?"

"Jake's new paralegal?" asked a voice that was cool and clipped. "Well, God bless you, dear. Do yourself a favor and have him microchipped so you can keep track of him. That would make life easier for all of us."

"Aah," Charlotte said.

"I don't suppose you know where the boy is right now, or why he's not answering his cell, do you? This is an emergency."

Lurching to her feet, Charlotte hurried to her door and peered around it into Jake's office. No Jake. With growing desperation, she glanced up and down the deserted hallway. Still no Jake.

"I don't see him in his office, so I'm assuming he just stepped out for a minute. Hopefully he'll be right back. But now you've got me worried. I hope no one's been injured or—"

"Injured?" Mrs. Hamilton emitted a scoffing little laugh. "It's worse than that. Although I'm going to break Jake's leg if he doesn't show up soon. No, it's the photo shoot today."

"Photo shoot?"

"Yes, dear, try to keep up. The whole family is here at Integrity—"

The Hamiltons' estate, Charlotte thought. Thank God she knew that much about the Hamilton dynasty.

"—getting ready for the photo shoot for *Eminence* magazine. They're interviewing me because of my charity work for foster children. You probably know all about the Tuck Me In Foundation already, right? Of course you do."

"Well, actually—"

"And you know about the charity gala in November, I'm sure. Have you got your ticket already? They're selling fast, so you'd better snap yours up if you haven't. They're only four hundred dollars."

Four hundred *U.S. dollars?*

Dumbfounded, Charlotte held the receiver away from her ear and stared at it. Did this woman not have the faintest idea how much the lowly staff members made here at Hamilton, Hamilton and Clark?

"Just make your check payable to the Tuck Me In Foundation."

"Of course," Charlotte murmured, figuring it didn't matter what she said anyway. Listening was clearly not Mrs. Hamilton's thing.

"Anyway, where is Jake? I need him here yesterday."

See? There was the proof. The woman had no idea how to listen.

"Like I said before, Mrs. Hamilton, I can't find Jake right now. I'm so sorry—"

Without warning, Jake walked in, holding two cups

of coffee and a paper bag from Starbucks. Apparently he'd heard that last sentence and realized who she was talking to, because his eyes widened and he shook his head in a violent *no*.

I'm not here, he mouthed.

Charlotte gave him a glare as reproachful as she could make it and then focused on the most pressing issue, which was getting off the phone with Mrs. Hamilton.

"—but as soon as I see him, I'll make sure he calls you. Have a wonderful day," Charlotte added.

"But—"

"Goodbye," Charlotte said sweetly, then hung up and folded her arms across her chest. "That was your mother, in case you're interested."

"I know." Jake put the bag on the desk and handed her one of the coffee cups. "Why do you think I didn't want to get on the phone? What was that all about, anyway?"

"She's having a conniption because apparently you're due at some big photo shoot. Like, right now."

Jake, who'd produced a pumpkin scone from the bag and had by now taken a huge bite, turned a nasty shade of green. "That's not today, is it?" he asked out of one corner of his overstuffed mouth.

She touched an index finger to her nose. "Bingo."

He groaned.

Charlotte laughed. "How bad could it be?"

He stared at her. "How can you ask me that, having just talked to my mother?"

"Well, you'd better get going. She's probably calling the police for an APB on you right now."

Her cell phone, which was in her jacket pocket, vibrated. Fishing it out, she took a quick glance at the display.

"I'm so sorry, Jake. I really need to take this."

Waving a hand, he took another bite of scone. "Go ahead."

Charlotte answered the phone by the third buzz. "Mom? Hi. How're you doing?"

"Oh, fine, honey," her mother said airily. "I just got home and I'm about to grab some lunch. Don't worry about me."

Charlotte strained her ears for the sounds of any unusual inflections in her mother's voice, but she sounded happy and energetic, thank goodness. "Do you have enough to eat? What about dinner—"

"Yes, Char. How are you?"

Charlotte surveyed Jake, who'd slouched into one of the visitors' chairs on the other side of her desk and was sipping his coffee, showing no signs of heading to the photo shoot anytime soon.

"I'm good. Well, except that Roger got called into surgery and bailed on me. Again. But Harry's asleep right now, and my boss is here, so I'd better try to get some work done. Gotta go. Love you—"

"Well, why don't I look after him?" Mom interjected.

"Why? Because you just got home from physical therapy three minutes ago. You should be taking a nap, not watching a hyperactive toddler."

Jake had, by now, demolished the scone and was wiping his fingers with a napkin. He hadn't bothered with any pretense of not listening to her conversation, and at these words, his face darkened with obvious concern.

Mom huffed loudly. "That's ridiculous. I feel fine right now, and I'll feel better if I get to see my grandson today. Bring him on over on your lunch break."

"But—"

"See you soon. Bye!"

Mom hung up.

Jake didn't waste any time nailing Charlotte with that penetrating gaze of his, the one that had a knack for stripping her bare. "Your mother's sick."

Sick.

Well, that was a succinct summary, although it didn't begin to cover the simmering terror that had become such a big part of their lives. Shrugging, she smoothed one side of her hair and focused on not looking as vulnerable as she suddenly felt.

"She's had heart issues. And a couple procedures."

"I'm sorry."

Charlotte tried to smile. "She seems pretty perky today, though. And she's back at work part-time. She's an elementary school teacher."

"That's noble work."

"I know. And she's good at it. I hope she's able to keep working for a while yet."

Thankfully, Jake seemed to sense that the topic was shaky ground for her. He got up and gave his hands a decisive clap. "Okay. Here's what we'll do. We'll drop

Harry off first and then head to Integrity. With any luck, we'll be there in less than an hour—"

Charlotte raised a hand.

He pointed to her. "Question in the back? Yes. Charlotte, go ahead."

"Excuse me, but what is this *we* business? I'm assuming you mean the royal *we,* right, because why would your paralegal go to some photo shoot with you?"

"So we can discuss our caseload and your duties," he said, as though this was the most natural proposition in the world. "I've got a big trial coming up in Pittsburgh soon. Lots of documents and witnesses for you to manage. Anything else?"

"Yes." Charlotte pointed to the TV. "I thought you wanted me to start with the deposition reviews."

"Oh, that can wait." He headed for the door. "Meet me in the reception area in five minutes."

Wow. Apparently you really needed to be able to turn on a dime around here.

"Wait," she called. "You forgot your bag. And thanks for the coffee, by the way."

He paused on the threshold. "That's for you. I thought you might like a pumpkin scone."

"Really?" Since she was starving, this news made her break into a thrilled and grateful grin as she peeked into the bag. "And what's this little doughnut with chocolate icing?"

"That's for Harry. If he ever wakes up. I figured my life wouldn't be worth living if I didn't bring him a treat, too."

"You were right." This unexpected thoughtfulness touched her squarely in the heart. As a mother and sometimes caretaker for her own mother, she spent a lot of her time thinking about the needs of other people.

It was rare that anyone thought about hers.

"Thank you," she said. "You're so sweet."

She'd expected a breezy reply. *It's nothing,* or, *I always bring treats for my paralegal on Mondays.*

So she was surprised when his expression clouded over, leaving troubled eyes and a grim jawline, as though she'd hit some invisible but tender nerve. They stared at each other for a quick second, and she felt the electrical impulses dance across her skin.

He looked away first. Nodding, he turned and walked out.

That was the dangerous thing about spending time—any time—with Jake, she thought, watching him go and knowing she'd feel the lingering thrill of awareness whether he was in the room with her or not.

They affected each other in unexpected but powerful ways.

Chapter 4

"This is it." Charlotte pulled her car up in front of a house that was little more than a white shoe box with a black roof. Surrounded by a chain-link fence and sporting weathered siding and green awnings over the windows, it looked as though it had seen its prime in the 1950s. But the lawn was lush and green, the flower pots were beautiful explosions of pink and white begonias, and the white wicker furniture on the minuscule porch looked freshly painted. "I'll be right back."

Ducking her head to avoid looking at Jake, she climbed out the driver's side and hurried to unstrap Harry from his seat in the back.

Jake watched her, wishing he could wave a wand and rescue her from her obvious embarrassment. He didn't care about how much money she and her mother had or didn't have.

He just wanted her to look at him again.

The awkwardness had started back at the firm's parking lot, where they'd had to decide whose car to take. For the first time in his overprivileged life, he'd felt… Was *ashamed* too strong a word?

No, he decided. It wasn't.

His car, which was in pride of place in one of the numbered spaces that belonged only to those members of the firm whose name began with *Ham*—and ended with—*ilton,* was a big-ass leased black BMW sedan, with every option a luxury car could sport, except a live-in chauffeur and masseuse. The payments were in the thou-a-month range, and he traded the thing in every year for the latest model.

And what did he use the car for? All the important things in life, such as going to work, the gym and the clubs. That was about it.

And what was Charlotte driving?

A Civic that had to be twelve years old if it was a day, and had the interior room for either a purse or a bag of groceries, but probably not both, and especially not with Harry's car seat and other accessories taking up so much space in the back.

And what did Charlotte use her ancient but pristine and clearly well-loved car for? Oh, nothing important, probably. Just driving her son around, driving to the firm, where she worked long hours for little pay, and driving to law school, because she wanted to improve her life.

Oh, and probably driving to church, because he had a feeling that was how she rolled.

He worked hard too, and he was a childless single man, which meant that he was free to accumulate all the expensive toys his heart had desired. But if he took a quick survey of five random people and asked them who was more deserving of the nice wheels, he had no doubt which way the vote would go.

And that shamed him.

He didn't like shame. He wasn't familiar with it, either, which was typical, he supposed, when your parents had money, paid for your education and generally cushioned you from life's rough edges.

Who had ever cushioned Charlotte? Anyone?

And how was this for irony: she was also ashamed of her circumstances. It was obvious in her flushed cheeks and ducked head, and the way she'd given her car a worried once-over when they had decided she should drive on account of the car seat in back, swiping at a crumb on the passenger seat before he got in, as though his ass was too good to sit on anything but the finest Corinthian leather.

Please.

"I'll just run Harry in," she said, slinging the drowsy boy over her shoulder and grabbing the diaper bag, "and then I'll be right— What're you doing?"

He climbed out of the car, ignoring the slight note of alarm in her voice. "I'm getting out."

Her eyes had gone wide. "I can see that. But why?"

"Because it's hard to meet your mother in the car," he told her.

"But—"

He understood her consternation. Typically, if he was presented with the option of meeting some woman's parent or, say, walking barefoot over red-hot coals, he'd start taking off his shoes and socks. But in Charlotte's case, he seemed to be ruled by his fierce curiosity. If he let this opportunity to learn more about her and her family slip by, he suspected he'd regret it for weeks to come.

Typically, he didn't feel regret.

Which was further proof that there was nothing typical about his reactions to Charlotte.

"Don't worry," he reassured her. "I know she just got home from physical therapy. I just want to say hi. Let's go."

Taking the heavy diaper bag off her arm—she shouldn't have to manage every freaking thing in life by herself—he strode up the walk. Her mother already had the door open and was waiting for them with her hands on her hips and a Martha Stewart white apron tied around her trim waist.

Wearing gym shoes and a powder-blue tracksuit with white stripes down the sides, she was an older and shorter version of Charlotte, which meant that she was bright-eyed and beautiful. He hadn't been sure what to expect when he had heard about the heart attack, but she was the picture of glowing health. Her chin-length hair was thick and sleekly black, except for a distinguished stripe of white down one side behind her ear, and her skin was nice and rosy.

"Well, who is this, come to see me?" she called with a delighted smile. He had the feeling that Charlotte—or anyone, for that matter—could show up, unannounced, with a busload of tourists expecting a steak and lobster dinner within the hour, and Mrs. Evans would still be this warm and welcoming. "If I'd known a handsome man was going to stop by, I'd've put on some lipstick."

Jake grinned, liking her already. He liked her even better when the thrilling scent of vanilla wafted out of the door and hit him in the nose.

"Jake Hamilton." He held out his hand and Mrs. Evans shook with a surprisingly firm, two-handed grip. "I work at Charlotte's firm. Nice to meet you."

"Let's see here," Mrs. Evans said, tapping an index finger to her lip and furrowing her brow. "Your name is Hamilton. Charlotte works at Hamilton, Hamilton and Clark. I'm going to go out on a limb and guess that you're one of the owners of the firm. Am I right?"

Jake opened his mouth to answer.

"Yes, you're right, Mama," Charlotte muttered, striding up the walk with Harry, who had by now cracked open his bleary eyes and was rubbing them with his fists. "He's one of my bosses, okay? Stop flirting."

"Does my flirting bother you, Jake?" Mrs. Evans asked.

"Not hardly," Jake told her, winking.

Charlotte, who didn't seem to care for the growing

camaraderie between him and her mother, scowled. Her obvious displeasure grew when Mrs. Evans all but snatched Harry out of her arms and smothered one of his fat cheeks with kisses while he squealed with delight.

"Will you let me carry this boy, please?" she asked her mother. "He's so heavy now, and I don't want you to get too tired."

Mrs. Evans just wheeled around, headed into the house and let the screen door slam shut in Charlotte's face.

"Talk to the hand, Charlotte," she said as she went. "Talk to the hand."

Charlotte stood there, glaring.

Chuckling, Jake edged past her and went inside.

The house surprised him. He'd expected doilies and crocheted afghans on every surface, but the style was sleek and airy, with taupe walls, white trim and black leather furniture arranged around a wall-mounted flat-screen TV that had as much square footage as the drive-in theater he went to as a kid.

The channel was turned to a congressional debate on C-SPAN.

"Can you believe those clowns in Washington, Jake?" Mrs. Evans demanded, heading for the up-to-date kitchen and plopping Harry down on the black granite countertop near the sink, where she proceeded to pull his thumb out of his mouth and help him wash his hands. "The economy is swirling right down the toilet, and those idiots—"

"Yeah, okay, Mama," Charlotte interjected. "Jake doesn't have the rest of the day to listen to one of your political diatribes. He's very busy, and we have to go, anyway, so thank you for taking Harry, and I'll see you— Oh, for crying out loud."

Jake had wandered into the kitchen and was also washing his hands while keeping one eye on the baked bounty cooling on one end of the counter.

"What's cooking?" he asked, never too proud to beg for a sweet treat.

"Cookies!" Harry clapped his tiny hands with unabashed glee. "Cookies, Mommy!"

"Little boys like you get cookies *after* they eat lunch," Charlotte told him.

"Nooo!"

Harry stiffened in Mrs. Evans's arms, bending over backward and kicking his feet in what looked like the beginning of one of those legendary toddler tantrums. Uh-oh, Jake thought, ready to run for cover if the situation deteriorated, but Charlotte, who was now in the kitchen, didn't look concerned.

"Nooo! No, no—"

"And little boys who throw temper tantrums," Charlotte continued calmly, "don't get any cookies at all."

Harry, apparently experiencing a change of heart, straightened midshriek and, sniffling, wiped the crocodile tears from his eyes.

Mrs. Evans answered Jake's question as though there'd been no interruption. "Charlotte and I are baking for the pastor's birthday luncheon on Wednesday—"

See? Church. He'd called that one, hadn't he?

"—and I'm in charge of the cookies. I put these together before I went to PT this morning and left them here to cool. So, these are shortbread, those are double chocolate chip, those down there are white chocolate macadamia and these here are peanut butter."

"The pastor's a lucky man," Jake told her, his mouth watering. "That's all I can say."

"Well, I need a taster. And I figured Charlotte wouldn't let anybody have any fun until after lunch, so I boiled up some hot dogs." She reached for a package of buns on the counter. "Does anyone here like hot dogs?"

"Me!" Jake and Harry cried together.

"I'll have two, if you have any extra," Jake added, turning to the fridge. "I'll get the ketchup and mustard—"

Harry scrunched his face and shook his head violently enough to cause a mild concussion. "No mustard. No mustard!"

"I'll just get some for me, little man." Jake grabbed the condiments from the shelf on the door. "I'm assuming you don't want any sweet relish, either."

"No way!"

"Alrighty, then," Jake said.

Jake accepted his loaded plate from Mrs. Evans and had just begun to doctor his dogs when Charlotte hit her limit. In an ominous sign, she crossed her arms over her chest and all but growled.

"Excuse me, Mr. Hamilton," she began.

"I like that," Jake told her around a mouthful. "You

can call me Mr. Hamilton or Boss. Whichever you prefer."

"In case you've forgotten, your mother is waiting for you at the photo shoot, so there's no time for your little meal. We need to go. I don't want her sending bounty hunters after us."

Jake waved a hand. "Relax. My mother is a drama queen."

"Yeah, but—"

"I'll deal with her when the time comes. Have you got any chips, Mrs. Evans?"

"In the pantry, honey," Mrs. Evans said, pointing. Then she handed Harry his hot dog. "Don't forget to say thank you, Harry."

"Thank you, Grammy," Harry said happily.

"Charlotte, honey, you should eat, too. I've got plenty."

Splitting her glare between Jake and her mother, Charlotte stalked to the fridge and rummaged around for something. Jake worked hard on not noticing the delicious curve of her ass as she did so.

"So, Mrs. Evans," Jake said, "I need to know so I don't get my hopes up. Are we limited to just one cookie?"

Mrs. Evans, now fixing her own hot dog, dismissed this idea with a laugh. "Of course not. You couldn't eat just one of my cookies. Have as many as you want. You, too, Harry."

"Yay!" Overwhelmed with his delight, Harry opened his mouth too wide, and a half-chewed hunk of hot dog fell out onto his lap. Without missing a beat, Harry picked it up, examined it in minute detail, then shoved it back into his mouth. "I want four cookies!"

Charlotte emerged from the fridge with a slice of pizza. "You get one cookie. Two at the most," she said before taking a bite.

Harry looked like he might protest, but Mrs. Evans saved him the trouble and patted him on his little leg. "You can have as many cookies as you want, Harry. Two cookies is the rule at Mommy's house. But what's the rule at Grammy's house?"

"No rules!"

"Hey!" Looking outraged, Charlotte turned on her mother. "Will you kindly not undermine—"

Jake's phone rang from his pocket. Everyone paused to look at him. Still chewing, he pulled it out, glanced at the display and handed it to Charlotte.

"Can you take care of this for me, Charlotte? Thanks."

"Is that part of my duties now?" Charlotte asked. "Answering your phone?"

"As needed, yeah."

"Oh. Okay." Charlotte took the phone and clicked it on. "Hello? Jake Hamilton's phone. Charlotte Evans speaking. May I help you?"

Jake's mother's voice came over the line, filling the kitchen as though she was right there with them.

"Excuse me, young lady, but did I or did I not ask for you to make sure my son showed up at the photo shoot? That was forty-five minutes ago. *Forty-five—*"

Flinching, Charlotte held the phone away from her ear and tried to get a word in. "Mrs. Hamilton, I did pass along the message—"

"—minutes, and I think it was a fairly simple request. So where is he? Did you tell him that he's holding up the whole—"

"Jake is on his way," Charlotte said sweetly but firmly, shooting him a furious look that made frost collect on his eyebrows. "Oops. I have another call coming in from court. I'm so sorry, but I have to take it."

"—photo shoot, and I can only stall the photographer for so long, so you need to tell Jake to get his butt—"

"Thanks, Mrs. Hamilton. Goodbye," Charlotte concluded, clicking off the phone.

It rang again immediately. Charlotte thrust it at Jake.

He checked the display—yep, Mama again—pocketed it, and chose a large peanut butter cookie. "These look great, Mrs. Evans."

"Thank you, dear."

"Why did you make *me* speak to your mother?" Charlotte shouted.

Jake shrugged, now selecting a white chocolate macadamia that seemed to have more chips in it than the others. "You answer my phone as needed. I *needed* you to answer the phone because it was my mother. It's not that hard, Char."

"Don't call me *Char*. You just told me two minutes ago that you'd handle your mother when the time came."

He stared at her outraged face—all flushed cheeks

and flashing eyes—and tried not to laugh. "That wasn't the time, was it?"

Charlotte seemed to choke on her anger.

Jake, knowing his life was probably at stake, kept his expression bland.

"Mommy's mad," Harry informed them all, glancing up from where he was using his fingers to swirl a drop of ketchup around on his plate. "Uh-oh."

Charlotte finally recovered. "We are leaving," she told Jake in a calm voice that nonetheless threatened dismemberment if he so much as thought about disobeying her. "You have one minute to say goodbye and get your cookies."

Deciding this was no time to push his luck, Jake turned to Mrs. Evans, who was eyeing him with speculative amusement, and gave her a smile and a quick peck on the cheek.

"It's great to meet you," he told her. Behind him, he could hear Charlotte grabbing Harry for a goodbye kiss and a tickle. The child's laughter was pleasing to his ears, like the trill of wind chimes in a gentle breeze. It was no real jolt to realize that he was sorry to leave in such a hurry and wouldn't mind coming back real soon. "Thanks for the delicious lunch."

Mrs. Evans held him at arm's length for a second, studying him with warmth and disarming perception. "You come back and see us, okay? Anytime."

"I'd like that."

"I mean it," Mrs. Evans warned.

"So do I."

Now for a goodbye to Harry, Jake thought, turning to the boy, who was perched on his mother's hip, grinning. He had a chocolate chip cookie in one hand, chocolate smudged down one dimpled chipmunk cheek, and a ring of ketchup around his mouth.

Jake smiled at him, feeling the hard tug of something in his chest.

If he'd seen a cuter kid in the last five years or so, he couldn't remember him or her right now.

"Bye, Harry," he told the boy, squeezing his little arm. "It was nice to meet you."

Harry giggled and lapsed into a shy routine that fooled no one. Ducking his head, he buried his face in Charlotte's neck and peered up at Jake from beneath his long lashes.

"Say *bye,*" Charlotte prompted him.

Harry raised one hand and gave a tiny wave.

Jake, feeling that tightness in his chest again, waved back and headed for the door.

"I like your fish," Harry called after him.

Jake paused, glancing over his shoulder at mother and son. They had their cheeks together now, and Harry had his hands around Charlotte's neck. They looked like a small but loving family, self-contained and utterly devoted to each other.

They looked…right.

"I like you, too," Jake said, low, and he'd meant to say it only to Harry, but his focus was inexorably drawn to Charlotte's guarded expression. In trying to look directly at her, though, he discovered that he couldn't. Too much unexpected stuff was churning up inside him, and the volume of it overwhelmed him. Maybe even scared him. What if she could see it? "I like you, too."

Maybe she should make it official and change her name to Alice, Charlotte thought as she finished up her call and, gasping, lowered the phone from her ear.

She'd definitely slipped through the rabbit hole today.

Jake—who'd wanted her free to take notes about their cases and make a couple of quick phone calls for him—was behind the wheel of her car now. This left her free to stare out the driver's-side window and gape at Integrity, the Hamilton family estate in the upscale suburb of West Mount Airy. Worse, the long approach up the circular drive gave her plenty of time to get nervous about meeting the legendary Hamiltons.

For one thing, her raggedy car, though paid for, was woefully unworthy of being in such elegant surroundings. In fact, the Hamiltons probably had a groundskeeper or some such person—someone whose duty it was to keep anything tacky, like, say, skunks, white pants after Labor Day, or cars older than two years, from marring the perfect splendor of the place. That person was probably already on the march, coming to expel the car from the premises. Immediately.

For another thing, she didn't belong there, either, and she had no faith in her ability to fake it for a couple hours. True, the family would be busy with posing and smiling for the photographer, and no one would probably notice her much anyway, but what would she do if they did? What would they talk about other than the weather? Mutual friends at the club? A recent vacation to Fiji? Fashion trends for the fall? Yeah, right. She could see it now: she could tell them about the latest sale at Target, and they could tell her what they'd seen on the runway during their annual pilgrimage to New York for fashion week.

Yeah. That wouldn't be awkward at all.

It wasn't that she thought that they were better than she was because they were rich and she was…less than rich. Significantly less than rich. It was just that she didn't feel as though she'd be spending the afternoon with her people.

This afternoon would be more like a turtle's visit to a bird's nest.

There was nothing wrong with a turtle, but it didn't belong up a tree.

And Charlotte sure as hell didn't belong here at Integrity.

The place was unbelievable. A stone mansion bred with a castle and set within a small-scale version of Central Park, it had leering gargoyles, a tennis court, a swimming pool, what looked like a greenhouse or conservatory and, yes, a turret.

Just in case anyone wanted to climb up there and drop boiling oil on the invading hordes during the next siege.

There was no telling how many bedrooms and bathrooms the thing had, and she was too demoralized to ask. All this well-landscaped architectural perfection put another dent in her battered self-esteem. Look at this place! Jake had grown up here. And where had she grown up? In a tiny house with a chain-link fence. Despite her family's tough circumstances after her father got sick and ultimately died from multiple sclerosis when she was seventeen, they'd scraped together enough money for her to go to college, and what had she done? Gotten pregnant by a jerk. Now she had another mouth to feed—a precious little mouth, yeah, but still an expensive mouth—and she was on the twenty-year plan for getting her law degree.

In short, Charlotte barely had a dime to her name, and her list of professional accomplishments included exactly two things thus far: graduating from college and getting into law school.

Whoop-de-freaking-do.

Jake, meanwhile, had graduated from Penn and Northwestern Law. He had a thriving legal practice and, she was guessing, plenty of money in the bank.

Bottom line? He belonged in this kind of high-end world. She didn't.

All of which reminded her that any sort of romantic relationship with him was doomed to failure on so many levels that she'd have better luck winning the gold medal for ski jumping in the next Winter Olympics than she would of becoming his lover and emerging unscathed.

And she needed that reminder. Because she was excruciatingly aware of his unyielding masculinity filling up her car, his easy charm with her mother, his unexpected kindness with Harry and, most of all, the prickling energy that crackled between them whenever they looked at each other.

Snap out of it, girl, she told herself as Jake slowed the car to a stop. This was no time to go all gooey inside over Jake. Nor was it time to lapse into any woe-is-me nonsense. Woe wasn't her. She had a job in a terrible economy, a healthy son and a loving mother who was on the mend.

All of which made Charlotte a lucky girl, and she intended to remember it.

Even when confronted with the Hamiltons, a family with enough money to give God a loan when He was running short on funds.

She gave a low whistle. "Nice house. Which room does the president stay in when he visits?"

Jake's profile tightened as he parallel parked at the end of a long string of luxury cars: Range Rover... Benz...Jaguar...and, yes, a red Ferrari.

Jake didn't seem to appreciate her humor. "It's ostentatious, I know. You don't need to remind me."

What?

"It's not ostentatious, Jake. It's beautiful. You're so fortunate to—"

Whoa. Apparently he didn't like that, either. Scowling, he climbed out, stalked around the hood to her side and opened the door for her. Which was, by the way, the first time in living memory that a man had opened a car door for her.

"Yeah, no. It's no accomplishment to be born into

a family that can give you every advantage in life. It's not exactly a reflection on me, you know?"

She slowly got out, picking her next words with the care of a jeweler searching through a pile of loose diamonds, hoping to find the flawless one.

"I didn't mean to offend you."

"You didn't," he snapped, heading for the front walk.

Putting a hand on his arm, she stopped him. "Don't brush me off, please. I'm not stupid. What did I say?"

With a rueful smile, he rubbed the top of his head before shoving both hands deep into his pants pockets. "Do you ever take a good look at your life?"

That surprised her. She felt her brows doing a slow creep toward her hairline. "Every now and then, yeah."

"Do you like what you see?"

Another surprise.

She took a second to remember all the issues she'd just been fretting about. And then she weighed them against her intentions, which were good, and her character, which was strong, and her heart, which was pure. Well, pure except for the part that occasionally wished she could snatch Roger's phone, throw it to the ground and stomp it to smithereens so that he'd be more engaged with his son. Let's call it ninety-percent pure.

"Yes," she told him. "Most of the time, I do like what I see."

A glimmer of admiration shone in his eyes. "Then you're a lucky woman."

She frowned with confusion. "And you're not a lucky man?"

"What have I ever accomplished in life?"

"A lot, from where I'm standing."

"There's a difference between not blowing the opportunities my parents handed me on a silver platter, and actually going out in the world and doing something, Charlotte," he said flatly.

"True," she conceded. "But it's never too late. You're not trapped where you are. If you want to do something important, then do it. What's stopping you?"

He cocked his head and narrowed his eyes, clearly thinking it over. "I don't know. Me, maybe."

"Well, you'd better get out of your own way, hadn't you?"

"And what should I do after that? Check and see if your crystal ball has the answer to that one for me, why don't you?"

Answers? Her? "You're barking up the wrong tree there," she said, laughing. "I hate to be the one to tell you. You need to figure it out for yourself. Give it some thought. The answer is probably right under your nose."

He paused, arrested, staring at her in that unnerving way of his—as though there was nothing inside her, not even a drop of blood or a cell's nucleus, that he couldn't see.

Waves of heat ran up her face, across her cheeks and converged on her scalp. "Well," she said, flustered. "We should go. Your family's waiting."

If he heard her, he gave no sign of it. For one second his eyes seemed to slide out of focus, and then, suddenly, a new light went on behind them, as though he was having an *aha* moment, and a significant one at that.

"Charlotte," he murmured, "you're a genius."

As always, praise, especially when she didn't know why she'd earned it, threw her out of whack. "I didn't—"

"Yeah," he countered. "You did. I have an idea for a project at the office. I'm going to talk to the powers-that-be about it after the photo shoot." He paused, unsmiling. "Thank you."

Mesmerized at being the focal point of all this unwavering attention, Charlotte felt her flush deepen until she could feel the hot rush of blood in her ears.

"Glad I could help."

He didn't answer.

"Your family," she said weakly, because they'd drifted closer to each other, almost within kissing range, and she needed to do something to break the spell between them.

It worked. Blinking, he looked around to the front door, and she had the feeling that he was reorienting himself to his surroundings.

"Let's go," he said grimly.

Chapter 5

They strode up to the front door. Charlotte took a few quick breaths and tried to get her mind right, which included not thinking about how much she wished she could kiss her boss. Was her face glowing purple? It still felt hot.

"Are you ready for this?"

There was a worried note in Jake's voice that made her grin. "Of course I'm ready for this. I know some of them from work. And they don't bite, do they?"

"They bite under the right circumstances," he said darkly. "Plus I'm not sure you've ever been confronted with this many Hamiltons at the same time. It seems like a terrible thing to do to a person. I don't want you demanding a raise or anything."

She shot him a sidelong grin as they climbed the stone steps to the porch. "I'm the single mother of a toddler boy, in case you've forgotten. Adults don't scare me."

"Foolish words, Charlotte," he said, raising his hand to knock. "I'm afraid you'll live to regret—"

Without warning, the huge front door swung open, and Charlotte found herself face-to-face with the woman who could only be Jeanette Hamilton, Jake's mother. Where else could he have gotten those intense brown eyes and sharp cheekbones?

Unfortunately, her mood seemed to be hovering somewhere between foul and murderous.

Straightening her spine, Mrs. Hamilton divided her flinty gaze between Charlotte and Jake. After smoothing her highlighted brown hair, she thinned her lipsticked mouth, narrowed her perfectly lined eyes and folded her arms across the front of her exquisite blue silk blouse. After a long moment, during which she seemed to struggle with the decision of whom to address first, she settled on Charlotte.

"Charlotte, I presume?" Extending her hand, she shook Charlotte's in a crushing grip. "I'll deal with you in a moment, dear."

That didn't sound good.

In a subtle gesture, Jake edged in front of Charlotte, blocking her from Mrs. Hamilton's displeasure. "No, you won't, Mother."

Looking supremely unconcerned, he kissed Mrs. Hamilton on her tight cheek, took Charlotte by the elbow and led her into the foyer. Charlotte tried—and failed—not to be awed, especially when a quick glance around revealed a spectacular staircase, vaulted ceiling with chandelier, antique sideboards, gilded mirrors, a couple curved benches, Persian rugs and long hallways spinning off to the left and right.

"If you want to be angry at anyone," Jake continued, "it should be me. I was running late. Sorry. What'd I miss?"

This apology didn't seem to cut it as far as Mrs. Hamilton was concerned. Closing the door behind them with a snap, she followed along, hot on their trail, heels clicking aggressively.

"Don't you try to weasel your way out of trouble with that lame apology, Jacob Hamilton the Third. You know very well that—"

"Oh, boy." Jacob Hamilton the Second, Jake's father and also a senior partner at the firm, strode through one of the arched doorways and came to a stop in front of them, eyes twinkling and voice filled with mock concern. It had been at least a couple months since Charlotte last saw him at the office, where their paths crossed periodically in the kitchen or on the elevator, and Charlotte was struck again by his youth and vigor. Both Jakes were tall, energetic and fit, although the older Jake's features were bracketed with lines that gave him a distinguished air, an effect that was intensified by his dark suit and red bow tie. "I see you've landed yourself in the doghouse already, JJ," Mr. Hamilton said, pulling Jake in for a back-thumping hug. "Nice going. I'll ask Cook to open up a can of Alpo for you. How does that sound?"

Laughing, Jake extricated himself from his father's grip and put a hand to the small of Charlotte's back, making sure she was included in the conversation. "You know, Pop, I'm not sure, but I think the world is still revolving on its axis even though we're a few minutes late. I could be wrong."

"Please do not be flip with me, young man." Mrs. Hamilton smoothed her hands over Jake's shoulders and gave his tie a tiny tug, straightening it. "This article is very important to me and my charity. *Eminence* is giving us the November cover story. Where else are we going to get that kind of exposure for free? And here you are, waltzing in like you haven't got a care in the—"

"Hello, Charlotte," Mr. Hamilton said, cutting smoothly across his wife and ignoring her tiny huff of disapproval. "Escape from the typing pool, did you?"

Charlotte nodded and smiled. "I did. Much to my surprise."

"And how's the boy of yours? Harry, right?" Mr. Hamilton asked. "You showed me his picture on your phone. That was at last year's Christmas party, wasn't it?"

Charlotte couldn't hide her surprise. "Wow. You've got a great memory. He's doing great, thanks."

Mr. Hamilton favored Charlotte with a benign wink. "You'll have a hard time finding a Hamilton man who doesn't remember a pretty face."

"Well, that's God's honest truth," Mrs. Hamilton muttered.

"Isn't that right, JJ?" Mr. Hamilton continued.

This harmless question seemed to throw Jake for a loop. Bright arcs of color crept over his cheeks as his gaze flickered to Charlotte before reverting to his father. He cleared his throat before answering.

"A pretty face is nice, yeah. A pretty face that belongs to an intriguing woman is unforgettable."

Arrested, Mr. Hamilton stared at his son, and Jake glanced down at his own shoes. Charlotte ignored the sudden prickly heat racing over her skin and refused to search Jake's comment for any hidden meaning.

Luckily, Mrs. Hamilton's singsong voice saved the moment from becoming awkward. "Oh, there you are, Azure. Did you two get some good shots of the house?"

A pretty young woman with a willowy frame and the height and confidence of Michelle Obama hurried down the hallway toward the group. Wearing a skirt and heels, she had a clipboard pressed to her chest and a photographer with about fifty pounds of equipment trailing after her.

"We did, indeed. I didn't realize you have a basketball court, too."

"Oh, we have a little bit of everything here at Integrity, dear. Let me introduce you to my son, Jake."

Smiling, the woman shook Jake's hand. "Great to meet you. I'm Azure Ellison. *Eminence* magazine. Thanks for letting us into your lovely home for the day."

Jake, always charming with the ladies, Charlotte

noted sourly, smiled, shrugged and shoved his hands into the pockets of his trousers. "We're thrilled to have you. I've got my own place, though. Integrity's only full-time residents these days are my parents and my sisters."

Jacob the Second clapped a hand on Jake's shoulder. "But you visit us whenever you can, don't you, son?"

"That's true," Jake agreed.

"We're going to take a few more pictures of the grounds," Azure said, steering her photographer to the front door. "We'll be back in just a minute."

Mrs. Hamilton, the picture of matriarchal grace, nodded and flashed a serene smile, reminding Charlotte of England's queen. "Of course, dear. Let us know if you need anything."

"Where is everybody?" Jake wondered aloud.

"They're doing what you should've done half an hour ago," Mrs. Hamilton informed him tartly, resuming her march down the hall. "They're in the conservatory, getting styled."

Jake gaped at her. "*Styled?* What the hell does that mean?"

Mrs. Hamilton pinched Jake's arm, making him yelp. Scowling, he rubbed the spot and glared at his mother. "Don't forget to put a twenty in the language jar on your way out," she said. "It's in the kitchen now. My charity thanks you for your donation. Here we are."

They'd arrived in the conservatory, which overlooked the stunning gardens in the back. Tiled and windowed, the space caught every available ray of sunlight, which explained the profusion of tropical plants in all directions. There were palms, orchids, birds of paradise and other spectacular specimens for which Charlotte didn't know the names.

At the moment, though, the room more closely resembled the chaotic backstage area at a fashion show Charlotte had once seen on a cable entertainment network. There was a makeup table with enough colorful products on it to adorn all the clowns the next time Ringling Bros. came to town. There was also a hair station and a rolling clothes rack that had dark suits—was that a tuxedo?—and various dresses and tops with beads, bangles and sequins in most of the colors of the rainbow.

Three or four stylists scurried back and forth with lint brushes, powder brushes and hairbrushes, looking for people to primp. Their manic energy was enough to make Charlotte want to take a Valium and lie down.

And then there were the Hamiltons, all of whom were lawyers at the firm—except for one cousin—and therefore familiar to her, if only in passing. The room was full of them.

They were sprawled on wrought-iron benches, leaning against pillars and congregated around the food table in the back. They all looked around at the arrival of this new group.

"What's up, people?" Jake asked no one in particular.

A chorus greeted him. "What's up, JJ? Jake! Why haven't you returned my phone calls, Jakey?"

Jake put that same protective hand on the small of

Charlotte's back as all the curious gazes swung around to her. "Everybody, this is my new paralegal, Charlotte Evans. This is her first day with me, so I'm counting on you folks to act like you have some sense. You should be able to fake it for a couple hours while she's here."

A round of jeers answered him, making Charlotte laugh.

"Charlotte, you know everybody from the office, right?" Jake pointed to his two handsome brothers, both of whom wore dark suits and slouched against the nearest pillar like bored princes. "The ugly one is Anthony. The smelly one is Marcus."

"Screw you, man," Anthony replied, but he had a smile for Charlotte. "Good to see you."

"Thank you for that vulgarity, Tony," Mrs. Hamilton called. "Kindly deposit your twenty dollars in the language jar on the way out."

Anthony rolled his eyes. Marcus guffawed.

"And I'll take twenty dollars from you as well, Marcus," Mrs. Hamilton added. "For general principles."

Both brothers glowered at their mother. They kept their mouths shut, though.

"And, Charlotte, you know my sisters, right?" Jake asked, pointing to two women—younger versions of Mrs. Hamilton, which made them elegant and beautiful—sitting on the nearest bench enjoying snacks. "Jillian is the bossy one and Marissa is the snippy one. But you probably know that from work already."

Marissa offered a vague smile and a wave. Jillian, meanwhile, took a carrot from the plate in her lap, lobbed it at Jake without comment, and hit him squarely in the forehead.

"Ow," Jake complained.

"Impressive aim," Charlotte said, trying to smother her laugh.

"Why, thank you, Charlotte," Jillian said, waving hello. "And by the way, you need to tell this jackass—"

"Twenty dollars from you, missy," Mrs. Hamilton interjected.

"—that being a paralegal doesn't include being dragged to photo shoots," Jillian went on, not dignifying her mother's command with a response. "I'm pretty sure that's not in your job description." She turned to her sister. "Are you going to let this pass without comment? I thought you'd be the first one to haul Jake to the woodshed for having an employee do something outside their normal duties. Hello? Marissa? I'm talking to you!"

Marissa, who'd lapsed into staring at the far wall and biting a fingernail, gave a start and looked around at Jillian. "What?"

"Your brother Jake, here—" Jillian began again.

Charlotte waved her hands, stopping her. "No one needs to go to the woodshed," she said quickly, before the dispute escalated. Anything was possible where siblings were concerned. "I'm glad to be out of the office for a while."

"Ha!" Jake flashed a smug smile at his sisters. "You got anything else to throw at me?"

"Yeah, actually." Standing, Marissa marched up to

Jake and pointed her finger in his face. Jake apparently took this as a bad sign, because he held up his hands in a gesture of surrender before she even got started. "What did you do to Rosalyn? She says you won't return her phone calls. Now she won't return *my* phone calls. What gives? What'd you do to her? Didn't I tell you to stay away from my friends?"

All movement in the room seemed to stop as everyone cocked their ears to hear Jake's response to this charge. Charlotte, feeling the strange twist of something unwelcome and ugly inside her, dropped her gaze so that no one would see her turmoil, but not before Jake glanced her way, as though he cared about her reaction to this accusation.

Please, Charlotte reminded herself. *As if.*

A guilty flush crept over Jake's cheeks but, to his credit, he stood his ground. "Let's talk about that later, Mar. Right now, I'm wondering why you look green around the gills. You sick?"

Charlotte had just been wondering the same thing; Marissa's color was definitely off. But apparently she was one of those never-admit-to-weakness types, because she swelled with outrage.

"First of all, there's nothing wrong with me, okay?" Marissa snapped. "Second, we'll talk about it now so I can figure out how to smooth things over with my friend."

"Yeah, JJ." Marcus, who was selecting a potato chip with great care, paused to regard Jake with wide-eyed interest. "Inquiring minds want to know."

"My mind is inquiring," Tony said. "What about your mind, Jill?"

"My mind is flat-out nosy," Jill said.

"Children, we do not have time for this," Mrs. Hamilton said.

"Sure we do," Mr. Hamilton said, one heavy brow quirked with amusement. "Jake?"

Lobbing an *I'll get you later* glare at Marissa, Jake shrugged and told his tale. "She called me after I ran into you ladies at the club."

"Right…?" Marissa said.

Jake's tone became more clipped. "We had drinks. It wasn't a love match, so I didn't present her with a red rose. She's called a couple more times, but I haven't called her back because I don't want to lead her on. End of story."

"I knew it!" Marissa cried with dark triumph. "You and your drive-by hookups do more damage—"

"We didn't hook up," Jake shouted. "That's what I'm trying to tell you."

"If you'd just keep it in your pants once in a while— Wait, *what?*" Marissa ran out of steam with a *whoosh.* "You…didn't hook up?"

"No." Unmistakable anger flashed in Jake's eyes. "And you owe me an apology, don't you think?"

"No. I don't think." Marissa hiked up her chin and went on the offensive. "With your track record, you can't blame me for assuming the worst."

"I'm waiting," Jake said, his jaw tight.

Marissa's anger stalled out. "Sorry," she muttered.

"For what?" Jake pressed.

"For impugning your pristine character. Happy now?"

"Not really." Jake's impenetrable gaze flickered to Charlotte, who had a tough time meeting it. A swoop of something that felt suspiciously like relief had lightened her insides, making her happy when she had no right to feel anything whatsoever when it came to Jake's love life. And she never would have any right, she added silently, because she seemed to need the reminder. "Maybe you should get your facts straight before you go around accusing people of—"

"Can we kindly focus on the matter at hand here?" Mrs. Hamilton's stern look touched all of her children before landing on Jake. "You need to get your makeup done so we can—"

"Excuse me?" Jake asked with open horror.

Mrs. Hamilton's eyes were chips of ice. "Your. Make. Up."

"Not in this lifetime," Jake said, striding away from the makeup table as though he feared a random blush would leap up and smear itself all over his face.

"But the lighting—"

"I'm not trying to make the cover of *GQ*." Jake checked his watch and pulled out his phone. "Can we get this show on the road? I've got work to do back at the office."

"Fine." Mrs. Hamilton, apparently deciding to choose her battles, waved a manicured hand at the clothes rack. "Just choose a suit and get changed."

Jake glanced up from scrolling through his emails. "I'm wearing a suit. See how my jacket and slacks match? Suit."

The other siblings snickered, but Mrs. Hamilton had apparently drawn her line in the sand and wouldn't budge. She pointed to the rack. "The selection includes Valentino and Tom Ford. Pick one."

Exasperation bled out of Jake's pores like sweat from a marathon runner. "This suit set me back two large, okay? I think it'll be fine."

Mrs. Hamilton didn't look impressed. "Who made it?"

Jake snorted. "How the hell would I know that?"

Quivering with indignation, Mrs. Hamilton turned her back on Jake and focused on her husband. "Will you please tell your stubborn and foulmouthed son," she began, barely getting the words past her locked jaw, "that he needs to change."

But she was fighting a losing battle. Mr. Hamilton was also now checking his email messages, and didn't want any part of the fracas. "The boy looks fine. Leave him alone."

Mrs. Hamilton and Jake squared off in identical fight-to-the-death postures, with their feet planted wide and their arms crossed over their chests. Charlotte watched and waited, giving them both even odds.

"No suit," Mrs. Hamilton said. "And an additional hundred for my charity jar."

"No suit and I'll give you fifty," Jake countered.

"Fifty and an hour of free legal service," Mrs. Hamilton said.

"An hour of my legal services for free? Are you insane? I don't even turn on my computer for less than five hundred an hour," Jake said, aghast.

Mrs. Hamilton, perhaps sensing victory, stood firm. "Take it or leave it."

Jake rolled his eyes. "Done. Shake."

Grim-faced, they shook.

Charlotte was trying to decide who had won and whether to laugh or not, when Mr. Hamilton caught her eye. One corner of his mouth was curled in a wry smile, so she figured it was safe to ask.

"Is this kind of thing normal around here?" she wondered aloud.

"Oh, yes," Mr. Hamilton assured her cheerfully. "You should see those two go at it when it's time to decide who gets to carve the turkey at Thanksgiving."

Charlotte was still laughing when a new group of Hamiltons—Philly was overflowing with Hamiltons— came into the room from the foyer.

First came Frank, Mr. Hamilton's brother and the other senior partner at Hamilton, Hamilton and Clark. There was no sign of his wife, Vanessa, though. Strange. But three of Frank's four adult children were there— Harper, Shawn and Benjamin. The three of them were lawyers at the firm. Charlotte had met them all in passing and liked what little she knew.

One thing was certain, though: those Hamiltons sure were a breathtaking group of folks. Had there ever been any unattractive children born into the Hamilton family? If so, what had happened to them? Had they been given up for adoption at birth?

The new batch of Hamiltons worked their way into the room. Greetings were called; hands were shaken; backs were slapped; Charlotte's presence was explained anew. She greeted everyone when it was her turn, but tried to fade into the background and stay out of the way while everyone got situated.

Her gaze was drawn, inexorably, to Jake. The strength of her curiosity mystified her, but she couldn't control it any more than she could control her hair on a rainy day. No detail about him was too small to escape her notice. Not the bright bursts of his laughter, the baritone of his voice or the boyish charm of his smile. Ten feet away, she watched him, hungry for every tiny bit of information that she could scoop up and swallow whole.

Which was why she saw what happened when the jostling crowd brought him face-to-face with his cousin Harper.

Jake's expression cooled into the below-zero range. His posture stiffened. His brows flattened. Harper, meanwhile, mirrored this response. They stared at each other with thin lips for a long and awkward moment that no one except Charlotte noticed.

Hugging each other the way they'd hugged everyone else was, apparently, out of the question. Hell, at the rate they were going, they'd be drawing swords and appointing seconds in a minute. Maybe the rest of the family should all run for cover before someone drew first blood.

Jake extended his hand and spoke first. Charlotte awarded him silent points for being the better man, especially when Harper gave him the kind of dubious look he'd probably use if Jake asked him to run his fingers over a spinning table saw.

"'S up, man?"

Harper shrugged, dropping his grip at the earliest possible opportunity. "Nothing. You?"

Jake met Harper's shrug with a shrug of his own, and raised him by crossing his arms over his chest in a hard-assed move. "Nothing. Where's Nelson? He couldn't make it?"

Yep, thought Charlotte. There went Harper, also crossing his hands over his chest. What was with those two? They were like two circling silverback gorillas.

"Nah. He's filming a commercial," Harper said. Nelson, Charlotte knew, was his brother, and the lone non-lawyer in the bunch.

"How long have you been with the firm, Charlotte?"

With an unpleasant start, Charlotte reconnected with the rest of the room and discovered Mrs. Hamilton standing next to her, following her line of sight with a speculative gleam in her eyes. This, of course, meant that she'd seen Charlotte staring at Jake. Assuming she had the normal amount of mother's intuition, this in turn meant that she now knew that Charlotte had a thing for Jake.

Not good.

"A couple of years," Charlotte replied.

"And do you enjoy working for the family?"

Uh-oh. They were wandering onto shaky ground.

"I do." Charlotte smiled. "Everyone's been very kind to me."

"Including Jake?"

Wow. Mrs. Hamilton wasn't one for subtle, was she? Jake came by that trait honestly, didn't he?

Nodding, Charlotte kept her face bland and willed herself not to flush. "Including Jake, yes. Although I just started working with him today. Before that, I was in the typing pool."

That disquieting gleam in Mrs. Hamilton's eyes intensified. Meeting her piercing gaze was like trying to discuss the weather with a hawk. "Is that right? And your typing was so exemplary that Jake promoted you to paralegal?"

Charlotte hesitated, trying to decide whether she was being insulted or not. "Actually, no. When he realized that I'm a law student, he decided I was qualified for more responsibilities."

"Interesting," Mrs. Hamilton murmured cryptically.

Interesting? What the hell was that supposed to mean?

Oh, but the interview didn't end there. There was more.

"I hope that you and Jake make a great legal team," Mrs. Hamilton said. "Don't let him get under your skin. He can be…a handful."

That was a thinly veiled warning, Charlotte decided.

The help wasn't supposed to mingle too much with the aristocracy. Plus, Mrs. Hamilton was probably more than shrewd enough to know that personal relationships between bosses and paralegals led, more often than not, to sexual harassment lawsuits when things went bad, as they inevitably did.

Charlotte got it.

Even so, her face burned with quiet humiliation, because this was nothing new.

Mrs. Hamilton didn't want someone like Charlotte involved with her son.

And Charlotte was sick and tired of being unwanted.

"Don't you worry about me, Mrs. Hamilton," Charlotte said, forcing a cool smile. "I'm a professional. I don't let *anyone* get under my skin."

Mrs. Hamilton's delicate brows rose. "Jake has a habit of getting under everyone's skin, dear— Oh, for heaven's sake."

This time, it was Charlotte's turn to follow Mrs. Hamilton's line of sight, and it didn't take long to figure out the problem. Jake and Harper were now in each other's faces, gesticulating, wild-eyed and pretty much breathing fire. In another moment or two, swords would be drawn, just as Charlotte had predicted. The only good things about the situation were that Charlotte couldn't see Azure at the moment—although how could the reporter fail to get wind of this little family feud?— and the men were keeping their voices low enough that it was impossible to hear what they were arguing about.

But they were both royally pissed off about something.

"Excuse me, Charlotte."

Mrs. Hamilton hurried over to the men and whispered a few stern words. Whereupon they wheeled apart, steam still trailing from their ears.

Jake, brows flattened in a heavy line, stalked straight over to Charlotte.

"Don't kill me," she cried.

That got him. His hard face eased a little, and dimples bracketed the corner of his mouth and quickly disappeared. "I can control my temper."

Since he was still glaring daggers at his cousin, Charlotte was not reassured. "You sure? I can hide the knives if you want."

His expression lightened a little bit more, and this time he treated her to the whole smile, which was a thing of beauty. "Duly noted. How're you doing? This is a lot of Hamiltons for a civilian to deal with. I probably need to put a letter of commendation in your personnel file or something."

"Works for me. You have a nice family. Except for Harper," she added quickly when she noticed Jake's frown deepening again. "Clearly he's a bad seed."

"Clearly."

"What a place to grow up. I've never seen anything like Integrity before. You're very fortunate to live such a charmed life."

"I've had blessings, yeah, but—" Jake's smile dimmed.

"What?" she asked, bemused. What could be wrong with growing up in paradise?

Shrugging, he ducked his head and ran a hand over his nape. "I guess it's ironic. You want to know what I was thinking earlier?"

"Yeah."

Jake looked up again, and their gazes connected. Somehow, in the course of this conversation, they'd drifted closer together again, as though they had secrets that could only be shared with each other. She told herself that it was because the room was noisy and crowded, but that was a lie, and she knew it.

The truth? Jake exerted a pull over her, and it felt primitive and overwhelming, like the tide's reaction to the moon.

"Tell me," she murmured, and the low note in her voice sounded way too intimate, not that she could control that, either.

"I was thinking that *you* grew up in a great house."

Charlotte stilled, staring at him.

The surprise must have been written all over her face, because he continued in a rush. "I know your mother's house is smaller than Integrity, and you probably didn't have the advantages growing up that I did."

"There's no *probably* about it. And I didn't have siblings, either."

"But you have a great mother. You have a *warm* mother. She lights up when you show up. She probably has time for you. Am I right? She probably can't love you hard enough, can she?"

"No," Charlotte agreed.

"Do you think I have that?"

Charlotte couldn't give a *yes* or *no,* although she'd seen enough of Mrs. Hamilton today to know the answer to that question.

"And you have a beautiful son," Jake went on.

Yeah, she did, but it was strange to hear Jake talking like this. The last thing she'd expected from this high-powered attorney and reputed player was a wistful tone when talking about Harry.

"Do you like kids?" she asked.

"You want me to be honest? I never thought much about kids one way or the other. But who wouldn't like Harry?"

Something tightened inside her chest. The unexpected emotion, naturally, sent her into defensive mode, which meant a joke. "Easy for you to say. You haven't seen him in the middle of a temper tantrum when you try to put his shoes on the correct feet."

Jake didn't say anything for a couple beats, which gave her a good long time to be blinded by the intensity of his brown eyes, which were speckled with black and streaked with gold.

"Just take the compliment, Charlotte," he said finally, low.

One syllable was all she could manage with her dry mouth. "Thanks."

"There was a lot of love in your mother's house this morning. I'm glad I got to see it."

Wow. Was there a sentimental core deep inside all that unyielding masculinity?

"Thanks," she said again.

"Okay, everyone." Breaking the spell between them with this harsh reminder that there were other people in the room with them, Azure marched in, clapping her hands. "Thanks for your patience. The light's good and we're all set, so let's saddle up. We'll take the first round of shots in the garden, okay?"

"You'd better go," Charlotte said.

The truth was, she was grateful for the interruption. The tension was growing between her and Jake, and she could see Harper out of the corner of her eye, watching their conversation with interest. That probably wasn't a good thing. She needed to get away from Jake for a little while and clear her head; she'd have had a tough time breathing if they'd talked for much longer.

"Don't ruin the shots," she warned Jake. "No inappropriate blinking. Make sure you don't have hot dog bits between your teeth. I'll stay out of the way and read the transcripts—"

But Jake, who seemed to have something more important on his mind, cut her off.

"I'm glad you're here, Charlotte," he said, unsmiling. "I'm really glad you're here."

Chapter 6

Jake was sitting at his desk and staring at his office wall, awash in thoughts of Charlotte, when she tapped on his door and poked her head in at around five-thirty that night. She had her purse slung over her shoulder, which led him to the conclusion that she was leaving for the day. Which meant that it would be tomorrow morning before he saw her again. Which meant that he was in for a long freaking night.

This whole lusting-after-his-employee thing was truly bad news. Because how could he stop lusting after her when he worked with her every day? And, conversely, how the hell could he stop working with her by, say, assigning her somewhere else in the firm, when his lust demanded that he see her whenever he could?

And here were the biggest questions of all: Why didn't this lust feel like the lust he'd felt for dozens of women before her? Why did it feel like…more? And why did *more* feel so terrifying? How was he supposed to extricate himself from this growing mess?

Can you say *screwed?*

"Hey," she said.

"Hey."

After the photo shoot, they'd driven back to the office in a silence that had felt awkward, if not downright painful, after the unexpected intimacy of their conversation. Then he'd retired to his office, she'd retired to hers, and, if he wasn't mistaken, they'd spent the rest of the afternoon avoiding each other. And there was another bit of irony for him: he could avoid her physically, but she was embedded deep in his head, tunneling through all of his thoughts like a mental mole working its way through his yard.

Too bad he couldn't eradicate her with some sort of pest control.

"If you don't need anything else," she said, "I'll just head out."

Head out. Yes. Good. Great. The sooner she left the better. Bye.

"I was just about to order some pizza," he announced, a total lie, because how could he eat when his gut was tied up in these boulder-sized knots? "Why don't you have some before you go? Least I can do for dragging you to Casa Hamilton."

"Oh." She blinked. Something crossed over her features, and he told himself it was regret. "I'd love to. But I need to rescue my mother from Harry. And I've got some reading to do tonight yet, so I'd better—"

"That's fine," he said quickly. Of course she needed to go home to her son and her studies. She wasn't the usual airhead he dated, whose most pressing concern after work was when to schedule her mani-pedi, and therefore had plenty of time to burn waiting for him to call. Charlotte was his employee. And she had responsibilities. Bottom line? She'd never be his, and he just needed to deal with it. "See you tomorrow, then."

"See you tomorrow."

But he could only let her turn and take one step away from his office before he found himself calling after her. "You've got Civ Pro this semester, right?"

She turned back. "Right."

"How's it going?"

"Not bad."

"Holler if I can help."

She brightened. "Really?"

"Of course. I need to put my high-priced legal education to some sort of use, don't I?"

"Okay, but I'll probably drive you crazy with stupid questions."

"Feel free. And no questions are stupid."

"You haven't heard mine yet, though, have you?"

He grinned. He'd been doing a lot of that since he met (well, noticed) Charlotte the other day. Enjoying himself. Laughing. And he knew he shouldn't, but he wanted more.

Where Charlotte was concerned?

More, more, MORE.

Which probably explained what he said next.

"I'll take a rain check on the pizza. Okay?"

She hesitated, turmoil darkening her eyes.

Which told him that he wasn't the only one struggling here, and that was a tiny comfort even if it wasn't enough to ease the ache of longing inside him.

"Okay."

"Mommy?"

At the sound of her son's voice Charlotte groaned. She was sitting at the kitchen table with her textbook, study guide, flash cards, notes and computer stacked in front of her in an overwhelming, yet oddly comforting, display. She'd had her head in her hands, resting her tired eyes for one quick second before she began tonight's reading, but now she looked up, knowing what she'd see.

Her son, who should have been asleep an hour and a half ago, stood in the doorway, regarding her with eyes that were wide and bleary.

Oh, for God's sake.

It was now—she checked her watch—nine-thirty. After leaving the office at the end of her extraordinary first day as Jake Hamilton's new paralegal, she'd picked up Harry, made a quick stop at the grocery store for some milk and endured Harry's embarrassing temper tantrum in the checkout line when she refused to buy him a bag of M&M's and let him eat it for dinner.

Once they had arrived home, she had made a quick supper of spaghetti and meatballs before giving Harry his bath and taking her own shower. This was followed by quiet snuggling on the sofa while watching the latest Elmo video for what had to be the billionth time, and then reading *Click, Clack, Moo* for, yes, the billionth time, too.

At that point, it was eight o'clock. Time for all two-and-a-half-year-olds to go to bed, right?

Not so much, apparently.

Harry, the love of her life, had climbed out of the crib to ask her to turn on his night-light, then to ask for water, despite the conspicuous presence of the full sippy cup on the table in his room and then for the inevitable trip to the bathroom for a follow-up pee, which was the only time all day he'd voluntarily tried to use the toilet. Now he'd reappeared for God-knew-what.

She, meanwhile, had sat there at the freaking kitchen table, fighting both sleep and her rising frustration, and tried, over and over again, to read the thirty pages of case law that they'd be discussing in class tomorrow night. The professor, who was making his way through the roster, hadn't called on her yet. Given her luck, this surely meant that, if she didn't get the reading finished tonight, he'd call on her tomorrow.

And she'd look like a dunce in front of everyone.

She loved her precious son. She really did.

But, honest to God, she was giving serious thought to trying to sell him on eBay. The keys, she figured, were a cute picture and a reasonable Buy-It-Now price.

It could work, right?

She stared at him, straining for patience.

"Did I, or did I not, ask you several times to stay in the crib?"

Harry nodded.

"You did hear that, right?"

Harry nodded.

"So your hearing is fine, then. Your listening ears are turned on and working."

Harry nodded.

"What is the issue, then? Because Mommy needs to study, and you keep interrupting. And that's making me upset."

"There's a monster under my bed."

Not that again. "I thought he was in the closet."

"That's the other monster. This is a new monster."

Great. Just what she needed on top of everything else. "A new monster?"

"Yeah. And he was behind the chair. But when I closed my eyes, he snuck under the bed."

"What does he look like?"

"Mean. He's got mean eyes and lots of sharp teeth."

Wonderful. Here was her reward for letting Harry watch an Animal Planet special about sharks the other day. "Well, what should we do?"

Harry pursed his lips and thought this over. "If he promises not to growl and stays under the bed, he can sleep in my bedroom. Because maybe he doesn't have a place to live."

Wow.

Just like that, the kid melted her tired and fed-up heart. And that was why she hadn't sold him online. Yet.

Plus, he was adorable.

He wore his footed blue flannel pajamas with, you guessed it, monsters on them. His green fleece blankie was hugged up close to his cheek for safekeeping, because, he'd previously explained, you couldn't leave a blankie on the bed and vulnerable to theft when there were monsters roaming about, and his little thumb was crinkled and wet from sucking. Plus, his curly hair was mussed, his cheeks were fat and he had that delicious clean-kid smell courtesy of his Johnson's Baby Lotion.

Yeah. Adorable.

"Come here, baby," she said, extending her hand to him. With a grateful smile, he scurried over to her, his feet scuffing on the tile, and scrambled into her lap for a quick hug. "Let's go talk to that monster and make sure he understands the rules."

"'Kay," Harry said sleepily, his head already drooping onto her shoulder.

Charlotte stood, cradling his solid weight against her chest, and was halfway down the hall when there was a quiet knock on her front door. She hesitated, her heart sinking, because she knew that knock, and there was only one person it could be. Maybe if she didn't answer and snuck down the hall to the bedroom, he'd get the message and go away.

More knocking, louder.

Harry's head came up, and he nailed her with eyes

that were now wide awake and shining with excitement. "Daddy! It's Daddy!"

Shit, shit, SHIT.

She felt cornered, because, while she may be the kind of mom who wanted to kick her baby daddy's butt on occasion, she wasn't the kind of mom who'd disappoint her son by keeping him from his loving father. So she surrendered to the inevitable.

"Shh," she told Harry as she changed course for the front door. Maybe if she kept him calm and quiet, it wouldn't be too much trouble to get him settled in after this unannounced visit. "Let's check the peephole and see who it is."

She checked. Yeah. Roger. The jackass.

Suppressing her huff of irritation for Harry's sake, she slid the chain and opened the door.

Roger, who now had a black leather jacket on over his scrubs and eyes sporting hollowed-out rings of exhaustion, came inside. "Hey."

"Daddy!"

Harry's glad cry saved Charlotte from having to answer. Which was a good thing because she wasn't feeling very civil at the moment.

Roger read it all in her face, though. His gaze skittered away to Harry and, clapping his hands, he pulled the boy out of her arms and settled him on his hip.

"How's my boy? What're you doing still awake, man? It's bedtime."

"Monsters," Harry said solemnly.

"I have an idea, Harry." Charlotte kept her eyes on

the boy, but her firm message was entirely for Roger. "Daddy can only stay for a minute, so why don't you let him talk to the monster and tuck you into bed. Okay?"

Harry beamed with approval. "Okay. Come on, Daddy."

With a last wary look over his shoulder at Charlotte, Roger headed for Harry's room at the end of the hallway. Charlotte, on the other hand, went into the living room, where she took out her seething anger on her decorative pillows, pounding them into submission on the chairs and sofa.

Roger came back a couple minutes later wearing that hangdog expression Charlotte couldn't believe she'd ever fallen for. "The kid couldn't keep his eyes open."

Charlotte saw no need for preliminaries or delays. "What are you doing here?"

Roger shrugged. "I didn't get my full time with Harry today. I wanted to say good-night on my way home."

Wow. Such paternal devotion. It really choked her up. Not.

The issue, she thought for the thousandth time, was that they lived two minutes from each other, a calculated decision they'd made as Harry's parents. They were close enough to make easy transfers of Harry back and forth, which was great. On the other hand, they were close enough that Roger thought he could drop in whenever he felt like it, which was both infuriating and, much as she hated to admit it, even to herself, harmful to her tender sensibilities.

Roger had been her first and only love. It was an immature and shaky college love, true, but she'd felt it, along with the heartbreak that came when it ended. It had taken her a long time to pick up the emotional pieces after their breakup, probably because Roger sent her signals that were so mixed, they might as well have been frapéed in a blender.

They were over. No, wait, they were on a break and needed to reevaluate. Good news! The evaluation led to a renewed period of recommitted bliss. Oh, but wait. On second thought—or fifth or sixth—they were over. For real.

She'd wanted things to work out with her first love. Wanted to make a family with Harry's father. Wanted not to be a failure at something so important to her son's future.

Now she just wanted everyone to stay in their own lane so she wouldn't have to go through that kind of heartache ever again. And she certainly couldn't do that when Roger showed up for these sort of unexpected visits.

The less she saw of Roger, the better.

"First of all," she said, keeping her voice low, because Harry was likely to turn up again at any time, and she never wanted him to see his parents arguing over him, "thanks for calling before you just showed up on my doorstep. I'm so thrilled that you respect my wishes when I ask you to give me the courtesy of a call so I can tell you if it's a good time or not."

Roger dropped his gaze and had the decency to look guilty, which helped smooth her ruffled feathers a little.

"Sorry. I just decided on the spur of the moment when I was driving past."

Of course he did, she thought, rolling her eyes. "Second, Harry's bedtime is eight o'clock, and you know it. When you show up like this, you run the risk of waking him up and getting him all hyped again."

A hint of satisfaction crossed over Roger's features, although he had sense enough not to let his face slide into an open smirk. "I didn't get him all hyped again tonight, did I? Looks like I helped get him settled in."

Unfortunately, she'd noticed. "Yeah, well, don't expect a round of applause from me. I need to study. The next time you show up unannounced, I'm going to ignore you. Whether Harry hears you at the door or not. We clear? Great. Buh-bye."

If he had some response to that, she didn't wait to hear it. Wheeling around, she hurried to the door and opened it, the better to speed his departure so she could focus on her studying.

Roger didn't move.

She gave him a pointed look over her shoulder and made a sweeping gesture toward the exit that he chose not to acknowledge. Still, she did her best to get rid of him.

"Buh-bye," she said again.

"I need to talk to you, Char."

His renewed use of the nickname he'd once spoken with such affection caused a sweet ache of nostalgia to ripple through her. But she was not going down that road with him. Not ever again.

"Don't call me Char. And I've already told you I need to study."

"It's important. Charlotte, please."

She paused, cursing herself for a fool. Then she closed the front door and went back into the living room, where they sat on the sofa.

"Thanks," he said.

She nodded.

The brief silence gave her time to notice a few troublesome details she'd been ignoring. Like the undercurrent of husky emotion running through his voice, and the thrumming tension between them, which didn't feel entirely hostile. Like how she wished she'd had time to throw on a robe, because all she wore was a cami and a pair of knit shorts, neither of which felt like much protection from Roger's sharp gaze as it flickered over her in a discreet inventory. Like how long it'd been since she'd had sex, and how the only partner she'd had since Roger had never been able to light her up the way Roger could.

Like how *really* long it'd been since she'd had sex.

Like how her body seemed increasingly dissatisfied with her self-imposed celibacy.

She cleared her throat, determined to keep this conversation on track. "What's up?"

"I've been thinking," he began.

"Yeah? I knew I smelled something burning."

He grinned; she grinned back; the air prickled with electricity.

But then a vivid flush of color ran over his cheeks, and she knew what was coming.

"Don't," she said quickly.

Too late. "I miss you, Char."

Her keen woman's brain understood the dangers of wading into these waters with him, but her girlish heart still had a corner reserved for the first and only man she'd loved.

If only she could cut out that corner and stomp it into oblivion.

"You don't miss me. You're just too busy to date right now, and you're probably a little lonely, and the booty calls I'm sure you have with your classmates and the nurses at the hospital aren't as thrilling as they once were—"

"I miss you, Charlotte."

"—and so you're thinking, *Hmm, I wonder what good old Charlotte is up to? Maybe she'd be up for round forty-seven of our dysfunctional relationship.* And so you came over here, and now you expect me to—"

Without warning, he cut her off by cupping her face in his hands and kissing her.

For a weak second or two, she responded. There was no way she couldn't. The sweet nostalgia of her long history with Roger, combined with her extended sexual drought and mixed in with her reawakening body, courtesy of her sizzling chemistry with Jake, added up to a match touched to the corner of an ancient piece of parchment.

There was a flame, yeah.

Their lips came together, sliding into familiar positions, and she felt the flickers of wanting. But when Roger groaned and angled her head to deepen the kiss, it was as if a brisk wind blew through her body and snuffed out that tiny flame.

She wanted, true, but she didn't want *this*.

She didn't want *him*.

She wanted a man she couldn't have.

And this poor substitute only sharpened her frustrated desire for Jake.

Breaking the kiss, she pulled back, put her hand to her mouth and worked hard not to make the situation worse by wiping Roger's taste away.

"I can't."

Roger's half-closed eyes were bright with lust and hope. He smoothed away the hair from her temples with gentle fingers and leaned in again, trying to resume the kiss. "You were, baby. You were."

"Stop."

Lunging to her feet, she paced away and then wheeled around, facing him. He, meanwhile, heaved one of those *you're-killing-me* sighs and flopped against the back of the sofa, covering his eyes with his arm.

Eventually, the tension level dipped enough for him to lower his arm and look at her again, his expression doleful. "I miss you," he said again. "I still want you."

There was that tug, again—the lure of the familiar

and the thrill of knowing she could still affect him after all this time. Underlying all of it was her bottomless and ongoing guilt over being unable to raise her son in a functioning two-parent family.

Didn't Harry deserve every advantage and blessing that she could give him?

Wait. What was she doing? Going back down that same stupid road *again?*

No way, José.

"It's over," she said, putting a lot more steel in her voice. "We can't go back again. And we've been getting along pretty well, except for when you bail out on taking Harry when you're supposed to. Why rock the boat?"

A crinkle worked its way down Roger's forehead as she spoke. By the end of her sentence, it was a full-fledged frown.

"Does this have to do with your new boss?"

The question came out of nowhere, swooping in and hitting her hard when she least expected it. "My new boss?" she spluttered. "What? No! Why would you ask such a ridiculous question?"

Roger wasn't buying it. "I saw the way he looked at you."

"Yeah, okay." Something inside her slammed into a brick wall, bringing her up against her limits. Maybe she couldn't control her attraction to Jake, but she sure as hell could control this deteriorating scene. "I don't know what you're talking about," she lied, "but it's late and I still need to study. And you and I are over. We had umpteen chances, and we never made it work, did we? So now it's time for both of us to move on."

"You can't move on with your *boss,* Charlotte. You're smarter than that."

She'd thought she was. But that was before Jake looked twice at her.

"It's none of your business." Marching to the door, she opened it for him. "Good night. Like I said, call first the next time. Thanks in advance for your cooperation."

Roger took his time grabbing his coat and crossing the room. When he finally started through the door, she heaved a tiny sigh of relief, but it turned out to be premature.

"I want you back," he murmured. "I don't think we're over. Not at all."

"What's going on?" Charlotte asked at the office one morning a couple weeks later.

Standing with his back to the doors, Jake wheeled around in the conference room, his pulse lapsing into an enthusiastic tap dance at the sound of her voice. Ridiculous as it sounded, even in the privacy of his own thoughts, he'd missed her since they both went home from work last night. A lot. Maybe he'd turned into a sappy love song, but his mind was full of Charlotte, to the exclusion of almost everything else. Since Starbucks Day, as he'd started thinking of it, she'd filled him up with sleepless nights full of manic wonderings.

Where was Charlotte now? At home? What'd Charlotte's home look like? Was she home and in bed? Did she sleep in the nude? On her side? Her belly? What kind of sheets did she have? Where was Harry?

Was Harry's punk-ass father there with them?

Since he didn't want his head to explode, he gave that thought a wide berth.

Some of his Charlotte wonderings were much more troublesome.

Did she think about him, even a little bit? Was it easy for her to work with him? Did she have any idea how much he wanted to touch her? Was longing for him eating her up on the inside the way it was eating him up, or was she blithely unaware and unconcerned about his growing fascination with her?

But the most troublesome Charlotte thought of all?

How long could he do the right and honorable thing and leave his employee alone?

Was he only fooling himself for thinking he could?

"Hey," he said.

He'd hoped to manage another syllable or two, something like, *How are you?* or *Come on in,* but the words danced in the distance, just out of his clumsy reach.

One corner of her mouth curled into a bemused smile, and the longing settled deep in his belly, forming a hard knot. Was she laughing at him? Did he look like an idiot? Why did this one woman regress him to a pimply sixth-grade nerd when he'd never been nervous around females, even when he was a sixth-grader?

Okay, Hamilton, he told himself. *You need to chill.*

But chilling was hard when she looked good enough to swallow in a single gulp. Today she wore a deep purple dress with ruffles. That, combined with some trick of the sunlight streaming in from the windows, made her more...vivid. Her gray eyes were bright, her cheeks rosy. Her hair gleamed, revealing streaks of red, gold and brown.

She was stunning, his new paralegal, and she wound him up tight.

He stepped aside, letting her through the French doors and all the way into the conference room. Grinning now, she brushed past, taking the breezy scent of her shampoo with her. Catching himself trying to identify the scent—it wasn't floral, but it wasn't quite fruity, either—he gave himself a swift mental slap upside the head.

Really? Now he was noticing the woman's shampoo? Come on, man.

Putting her hands on her hips, Charlotte watched as the interior designer held up her paint cards to the wall and murmured with her assistant. Then her gaze swung around to the other side of the huge room, where the architect was taking measurements.

"What're you doing to the conference room?" Charlotte demanded.

"Recommissioning it," Jake told her. "No one ever uses this one anyway."

"Yeah?" Charlotte edged aside as a pair of workers started grabbing the tall chairs surrounding the table and moving them into the hall. "Recommissioning it into what?"

"A day care for employees' kids," he told her.

Those bright eyes of hers widened, and her mouth formed a round *O* of surprise. "A...day care?"

"Well...yeah."

Ducking his head, he ran a hand over his scalp and questioned his own motives. The feeling was equally unfamiliar and uncomfortable. After his Charlotte-inspired epiphany the other week, right before they went inside Integrity for the photo shoot, he'd made a few quick plans and run them by his father and uncle. Not only had they wholeheartedly approved, they'd clapped him on the back and congratulated him on his sudden philanthropic impulses.

Little did they know that a fierce desire to help Charlotte was behind the day-care idea. If it accidentally benefitted the other employees as well, so much the better.

Which led him to shine a bright and unflattering light on his character.

Was a good work still a good work if you did it with mixed motives?

And now, with Charlotte looking at him as though he was responsible for the stars' diamond glitter in the night skies, could he bring himself to care?

"But—" she said faintly.

She trailed off, looking too stunned to continue.

Her overwhelmed silence made him blather.

"You gave me the idea before the photo shoot, re-member? And I got the go-ahead from the higher-ups. Made a few phone calls. Now we're getting things started."

Eyeballing the bustle of activity, which, with the addition of a pair of electricians, was now beginning to look like ground zero at some high-rise construction site, she got right to the heart of this understatement.

"A few phone calls?"

He hurried on with his explanation. "We've got five parents here—including a couple dads—with a total of twelve kids under school age. Well, that's the number I've counted so far. Then we've got four parents with a total of five teenage daughters who are at loose ends either before or after school. Why not put them together? We can hire a couple full-time day-care workers, and the teenagers can be volunteer assistants when they have the time. Some of them even need volunteer credits to graduate from high school, so I figure this'll kill about ten birds with one stone. We'll make the employees' lives easier, because they won't have the day-care hassles and the travel time issues with picking kids up and dropping them off, so we should get more productivity out of them. Oh, and it'll be a free benefit of working here, of course. So the employees will save money that way. We have to get state licensing, too, but how hard could that be with all the lawyers we have around here? I'm thinking we can be up and running by—"

Her hand on his arm put a stop to his diarrhea of the mouth, thank God.

"You did this?" she asked, disbelieving.

Jokes came easily to him when he was flustered. "What? Spent the firm's money?"

"I'm serious. Do you know how many lives this will change? Including mine?"

"I don't know about all that. I just, you know—"

Her eyes changed color on him, turning a flinty gray. "Are you telling me this won't change my life?"

"Well…no, but—"

"This'll save me about a thousand dollars a month. Do you know how much money that is to me?" She was gathering steam now, beaming at him with a megawatt smile that felt like more than reward enough for any little day-care idea he'd had. "It'll save wear and tear on my car. And gas. And travel time, which means I'll have way more time to study. And the money I save on day care, I can use on classes. With my promotion, I figure I'll have my J.D. by, say, the end of the month, at the very latest."

He laughed.

She sobered. "Thank you, Jake. I can't even—" She shrugged, swallowing hard. And if he didn't know better, he'd say he saw the sparkle of tears in her eyes before she blinked them back. "Thank you."

Oblivious to the commotion all around them, she stepped forward, hugging him.

For one arrested moment, the unexpected contact froze him inside his own body, and he couldn't, for the life of him, figure out what he should do.

But then instinct took over.

His arms came up and tightened around her, hard, pulling her closer until their thighs were pressed together and he could feel the hot pressure points where her firm breasts met the wall of his chest. The rightness of it—the exquisite perfection—nearly choked him, as did the soft sigh of her breath.

For one millisecond, he let his eyes roll closed—maybe one of the worker bees saw them, but screw it—and just experienced everything about her: the supple body under the silky dress, the sweet warmth of her skin, the satin brush of her hair against the backs of his fingers.

And then he pulled back, setting her aside while he was still capable of letting her go.

Too undone to look her in the eye, he put his hands on his hips and strode a few steps away, making a project of studying the room. In his peripheral vision, he saw her wrap her arms around herself and look in some other direction as well, as though she also thought eye contact wouldn't be prudent at this sexually charged juncture.

Unless he was the only one who thought it was sexually charged—a thought that made him want to throw back his head and howl like a young werewolf at his first full moon.

"So, uh—" He paused, clearing his husky throat. "We're going to need a fair amount of input from the parents on staff. What kind of equipment we'll need, and a committee to help with the interview process so we make sure we get top-quality people." He scrubbed a hand over his chin, wishing his body wasn't quite so violently alive right now. It would sure be easier to think a thought or two. "Maybe we should just, uh, go ahead and form a permanent day-care committee to handle the whole project. What do you think?"

Silence.

"Charlotte?"

The sound of her name seemed to register with her. Starting, she ran a hand through her hair, messing it up, blinked away the glazed look in her eyes and flashed a smile that was bright but looked a little forced.

"Committee? That's a, uh, great idea. So I'd like to, uh, be your first volunteer. If that's okay, I mean. Because I don't want to…you know, take too much time away from my regular duties."

"Good idea. Your boss can be a real SOB."

"My boss is a great guy." The sudden fervency in her voice surprised him and seemed to embarrass her. A vivid flush gathered in her cheeks and quickly spread over her entire face, but she didn't back away from what she'd said. "And a surprising guy," she added softly.

He stared at her, not knowing what to make of this assessment, or of the sudden wild hope thudding in his chest. "Charlotte," he began.

"Why did you do it?"

For you. I did it all for you.

The words were right there, waiting to come out, but it wasn't right to say them when he'd promised his behavior would be strictly professional. So he swallowed them back, creating a knot of misery in his throat.

"It was the right thing to do."

"For your employees?" she asked, and he had the

eerie feeling that she was testing him, that she knew he was lying.

He stared her straight in the face. "I'd do anything for...my employees."

Her breath hitched sharply, and she looked away from him.

As though she understood exactly what he wasn't saying.

As though the heat of his desire had reached out and burned her.

Chapter 7

About an hour later, after they'd both had a chance to decompress a little, Jake poked his head in her office. He was afraid he'd crossed a line somehow—afraid they weren't cool anymore—and had to make sure that he hadn't rattled her too much.

"Got a minute?" he asked.

"Absolutely."

Her welcoming smile was the same as always, which should have been a relief. It wasn't. Was she always so cool and collected? Was he making any sort of a dent in her self-protective shell? Why did sticking to his gentlemanly behavior feel like it was eating up years of his life?

"So did you get your reading done last night?"

She rolled her eyes. "Barely. Your little friend Harry—"

"Your son, Harry?"

"Yeah. He was a real pain in the rear last night. He did not want to go to bed. That's becoming a real habit with him lately. And then he wanted to call his father and say good-night. Again. He likes speaking on the phone."

"His father, eh?" Jake couldn't stop his scowl, nor could he keep the sour note out of his voice.

"Umm." She ducked her head, refusing to elaborate while he slumped into one of her visitor's chairs. "What about you? Did you have a good night?"

He frowned, thinking of the pizza he'd ordered—his third in the last ten days or so—the mindless channel-surfing he'd done and the solitary sleeping he'd had in his big bed.

"The usual," he said, trying to make *the usual* sound as though it was remotely interesting. "Oh, and I've been meaning to mention the barbecue at my house on Saturday. It's a thing I have every year for the staff I work most closely with and their families."

"Did you say barbecue? As in ribs?"

"Smoked ribs," he added to sweeten the deal. "You haven't lived until you've had my smoked ribs."

"Strong words."

"You'll see. It's a great time. Bring Harry and your mother. Like I said, it's for families. Oh, and I have a pool, if anyone wants to swim."

His mind flashed ahead a couple steps, to Charlotte

in the kind of black string bikini that she probably didn't even own, and he had to back away from the image before it scorched his eyebrows.

"We'll be there." She smiled like she was looking forward to it. "Thanks."

She'd be there. An unreasonable wave of pleasure swelled inside him, suffusing the world with brighter colors, more sunshine and, for all he knew, rainbows and unicorns.

He was truly becoming an idiot where this woman was concerned.

Sad.

"Maybe we should talk about the day care," Jake commented.

"Right." She grabbed a legal pad and started jotting things on it. "So I think the most important issue with the day care will be the licensing. Which lawyer did you say is— Whoa, what's all this?"

Something past his shoulder had caught her attention. Jake slung his arm over the back of the chair and twisted at the waist in time to see the receptionist stride in with a wide smile and a giant gold box of Godiva chocolates with a big red ribbon tied around it.

"Surprise, Charlotte!" the receptionist sang. "These are for you!"

"Oh, no," Charlotte cried, holding her palms up in a stop-where-you-are gesture. "Don't you bring that in here. That's got to be ten pounds of truffles, and I'll eat all of them before lunch. Do not put them on my desk."

Laughing, the receptionist deposited the box right in front of Charlotte, who gave it a baleful glare.

"Really?" Charlotte asked sourly. "Where did this come from, anyway?"

"A very handsome doctor just delivered them for you. And there's a card," she called, sweeping back out of the room.

A very handsome doctor.

Jealousy hit Jake like a brass-knuckled punch, knocking away the sweet thrill of being with Charlotte and leaving only a nasty taste in his mouth. So there was, at the very least, some unresolved business between Charlotte and Dr. Punk, and here was the proof. Maybe it was only that baby daddy still wanted her, and who could blame him for that?

A worse possibility was that they were still together, still working on constructing the perfect little family for Harry who, of course, deserved nothing less.

And the most sickening part of all? Dr. Jackass was a competitor for Charlotte's affections, and there wasn't a damn thing Jake could do about it. Jake couldn't even enter the freaking playing field, because he was her boss and, in addition to not wanting sexual harassment complaints lodged against him, he wanted to do the right thing by Charlotte. She needed this job and the opportunities he could give her and he was determined not to make her complicated life any messier.

And where the hell had that noble impulse come from?

Were more noble impulses lurking in the background, waiting to sneak up on him?

He stared at the top of Charlotte's downturned head, trying to decide what to do.

This was a tricky moment, and he knew it. Bosses had no business asking about the personal lives of their employees, so he needed to sit tight and keep his big mouth shut.

"Nice gift," he said tartly.

"Yep," Charlotte agreed. She had a white envelope between her thumb and forefinger, and she didn't look too anxious to open it and see whatever gooey love message was inside. "I love chocolates." Blinking, she seemed to emerge from her thoughts. "You love sweets, too." She slid the box across the desk to him. "Help yourself. I can't eat all this alone."

"Nope." He'd sooner eat a bacon, lettuce and turd sandwich than enjoy one of those tainted chocolates from Dr. Whatsisname. But he didn't need to be rude about it, did he? "Thanks."

Nodding, she pushed the candy and card to a far corner and picked up her pen again. "Okay. We should probably get back to work."

Back to work. Yeah. Good idea. Work was a safe topic. He opened his mouth to agree with her.

"You don't look too happy with your truffles," he noted instead.

She shrugged and waved a hand. "It's nothing."

"What's the issue?"

"You don't really want to hear about my little problems, do you?"

Hell, yeah.

"I'm a good listener," Jake said.

This was not, strictly speaking, the absolute truth. It wasn't even mostly true, come to think of it. He had a short attention span for other people's problems, especially when they lapsed into whining. Probably because he was good at slicing through layers of bullshit and getting to the heart of issues. When people didn't want to engage in reasoned analysis and then make sound decisions, he quickly tuned out. He didn't have time for wishy-washy waffling.

In Charlotte's case, however, he was willing to keep his butt plastered to this chair and listen for as long as she had things to tell him. And he knew her well enough by now to know she didn't whine.

"Roger and I have different, uh, ideas about the, uh, direction of our relationship. He wants to try again. I'm all tried out. The end. And that's probably way more than you ever wanted to hear about your paralegal's personal life, so I won't bore you any—"

"Why are you all tried out?"

Jake congratulated himself on the nonchalance of his tone. Listening to him, you'd never know that his whole body felt like it was crammed inside his tight throat, making it impossible for him to breathe.

Charlotte hesitated, her gray eyes stormy and troubled. "I have no idea why I'm discussing this with you."

Jake was smart enough to keep his mouth shut and wait.

"I guess," Charlotte continued softly, running a hand through her hair, "it's because I never felt like Roger met me halfway. I was more invested than he was. I gave more of myself than he did. His wishes were always more important than mine were. His education and career. His life. I felt…" A frown grooved down her forehead as she searched for the right word.

"Marginalized?"

Her expression cleared. "Marginalized. Yes. Exactly. And then, after a while, I just stopped caring."

"I see."

One edge of her mouth curled with cynical amusement, and she gave him a look. "Well? Don't you have a defense to make on behalf of the International Brotherhood of Career Men? Don't tell me you're not a card-carrying member?"

He loved her sense of humor. "I am a card-carrying member, yeah, but I'm not going to defend…Roger." He forced out the name, as though he were ejecting a mouthful of dirt.

"Why not?"

"Any man who wouldn't move heaven and earth to make things work with you," he quietly told her, "is too stupid to live."

Ah, shit.

Where had that come from?

He'd meant to say something generic, like, *Love shouldn't hurt,* or, *A man should put his woman first,* or, *I'm sure there's someone better out there for you.*

He certainly hadn't meant to sound like *he* would move heaven and earth to make things work with her.

But the damage was done. Apparently she'd heard

the note of longing in his voice or seen something in the way he was looking at her, because she stilled and watched him, her eyes bright and her color high. After a couple of exquisitely pregnant beats, she opened her mouth, seemed to think better of it, and closed it again.

"What?" he asked.

"Maybe Roger and I both needed to do some more growing up. What about that possibility?"

Did she think that would make him back away from his pronouncement about Roger?

"You look pretty grown to me." He hesitated before making a quick decision. At this late point in the conversation he figured, what the hell, he may as well go for it. "He's not the right man for you, and you're smart enough to know it."

"How do you know?"

"I know."

This, for some reason, seemed to irritate her. Her jaw firmed and her brows lowered, giving her a flinty expression. "What makes you an expert on all this, pray tell? Have you ever moved heaven and earth for a woman?"

"No," he admitted.

A gleam of grim triumph appeared in her eyes.

"But when the woman and the time are right," he continued, unsmiling, in another bewildering burst of *where-the-hell-did-that-come-from?*, "you better believe that I will."

Silence fell, and it was vibrating and tense, full of the chemistry between them.

The moment's intensity was too much for her, apparently.

She abruptly turned away from him, looking at her computer screen and breathing hard with some emotion he would have cashed in his retirement fund to discover.

Suddenly her phone beeped and the receptionist's voice came over the line. "Charlotte? Jake's not still in there with you, is he?"

Charlotte brightened. She was probably grateful for the interruption. He wasn't.

"I'm here," he said.

"Line eight's for you."

He didn't care about any freaking phone call, but, on the other hand, he was at work and should probably at least pretend he was working.

"Put it through. Can you put it on speaker for me, Charlotte? Thanks."

"Jake Hamilton," he said when the call came through.

"Hey, stranger," answered a woman's voice in a seductive coo that scraped over his nerves like glass chards. "Why haven't I seen you lately? Are you punishing me?"

Shit. Shit, shit, SHIT.

Jake lunged up and across Charlotte's desk for the receiver so he could get this call off speaker, painfully aware of her thinning lips and the patches of angry red on her cheeks as she spun her chair around to her cabinet. She jerked it open and rummaged through some files, her face averted.

"Hey," he said in the same professional voice he used

when clients called. "I'm in a meeting, so this really isn't a good time for me."

Since he didn't recognize the voice and couldn't see the phone's display from where he was standing, he had no idea who he was talking to. A woman he'd done the nasty with, clearly, but which one?

And wasn't that a pathetic and painful commentary on the state of his personal life?

"Oh, okay," the woman said in his ear. "Well, call me back later, okay? I was really hoping we could hook up for dinner at my apartment one day this week. I have a new recipe I want to try out on you."

Jake floundered.

He still had no clue who he was talking to.

Selita? Trish? It definitely wasn't Janay…

"That's not going to work for me," he said, holding on tightly to his professional voice. "Sorry."

"Oh," the woman said, sounding disappointed. "Well, call me anyway, and we can set something up for next week."

"Well—"

Eyeballing the top of Charlotte's head, he decided there was no hope for it. He couldn't see the phone's display, so he'd have to ask the woman's name. He could hang up and never call the woman back, but since his orange-juice bath at Starbucks, he'd become aware that his previous behavior with women *may* have been some-what callous. Better to just call the woman back, have the awkward conversation and tell her he that wouldn't be seeing her again rather than leave her wondering.

So he would, for once, do the right thing, even if it made him look bad—well, terrible—in front of Charlotte.

But before he did the right thing, he had to figure out who the hell he was talking to.

"I'm so sorry," he said gently, wishing he could be doing something less painful, like, say, passing kidney stones, "but I didn't catch your voice."

Charlotte, who was making a real project out of looking for God-knew-what in her file drawer, made a soft and indistinct sound of disbelief.

In his ear, meanwhile, he could almost hear the blood as it dropped from the stab wound he'd given the poor caller.

"It's Ella."

Ella! The woman he'd met at a Sixers game last winter!

They'd hooked up for a while. In fact, she'd made him a truly delicious mushroom risotto a while ago, a meal that was coming back to him with more clarity than either her face or, frankly, the sex afterward.

But still, her voice should have rung a bell.

"And don't bother calling me back," Ella snapped. *Click.*

Yeah, okay. He'd deserved that.

Without a word, he passed the phone across to Charlotte, who, using two fingers, dropped it back onto the base as though it had been contaminated with a nasty hybrid of Ebola and tuberculosis.

"Well," she said, still not looking at him, "I'd better let you get back to work."

"We were talking," he reminded her.

"I think we were finished, don't you?"

Something about her sudden crisp authority galled him. Who was the boss around here, anyway? "No. I don't think."

That got her. Her head came up and she used her sharp voice with surgical precision, slicing off a nice strip of his flesh. "Let me rephrase. I'm finished listening to interpersonal advice from a man who probably needs a color-coded Excel spreadsheet to keep track of the women in his life."

This well-earned dig nonetheless made him fume with irritation, but then it hit him. There was something about the haughty angle of her chin and the steely flash in her eyes....

"You're jealous," he said, incredulous.

"Please," she snapped. "Your head really should double as one of the Macy's Thanksgiving Day Parade floats. It's overinflated enough."

"You are."

Charlotte swelled with indignation. "Even if I were stupid enough to be attracted to my boss—which I'm not," she added quickly, probably because she saw the wild glimmer of hope in his eyes, "I'd never be stupid enough to get involved with someone who thinks women are interchangeable—"

"I'm jealous, too."

She snapped her mouth shut and froze. He couldn't

blame her. The three words scared him, proving that he was further gone over Charlotte than he'd feared. In his entire rich and varied dating life, he'd never been jealous over a woman, much less admitted it to her.

"At the thought of some other man sending you candy?" he continued with an embarrassingly husky note in his voice. "You'd better believe I'm jealous."

Across the width of the desk, they stared at each other while the silence seethed around them. After several long beats, she tried to joke away his confession.

"You're not jealous. It's just a shock to your system to stumble across a woman who tells you no."

If only that were it.

"If my system is shocked," he said, holding her gaze and doling out his words slowly, probably because he was only just discovering, right this second, how much truth was in them, "it's because I'm discovering that women aren't fungible after all."

A flare of unmistakable panic widened her eyes.

And then, without a word, she got up and hurried out, leaving her own office to escape him.

Chapter 8

Wow, thought Charlotte.

"Wow," breathed Mama.

"Is this a house?" asked Harry, who was holding both their hands and walking between them as they edged around all the parked cars lining the driveway.

"This is, in fact, a house," Charlotte assured him. "Mr. Hamilton's house."

"It looks like a glass box!" Harry said.

It did indeed. A very expensive glass box. Wedged into a leafy green hillside and surrounded by mature trees, Jake's house was a marvel of modern architecture that consisted, as far as Charlotte could tell, entirely of windows. It was so sparse and masculine that just looking at it was like mainlining testosterone. Even the landscaping was strong and masculine, with bold profusions of grasses and shrubs in different colors and textures.

The consummate bachelor pad, Charlotte thought, irritated.

It figured.

They reached the massive front door, where Charlotte hesitated. She and Mama, both wide-eyed with awed appreciation, exchanged a glance across the top of Harry's head.

"Should we go around to the pool?" Charlotte asked. "I hear voices back there."

The door swung open, and there stood Jake.

His gaze swept the three of them before landing on Charlotte and lingering in a discreet once-over that touched on her filmy peach cotton dress, bare arms and legs, and strappy sandals.

"Hey," he said, beaming as though he'd discovered a four-foot-high stack of shrink-wrapped hundred-dollar bills on his porch. "Welcome."

Charlotte made a token attempt to ignore the kick of adrenaline that pumped through her at such a warm greeting, but it was impossible. Quiet pleasure flushed through her veins, adding to the sun's warmth on her skin.

Idiotic, right?

Part of her issue was that, by some unspoken agreement, they'd avoided each other as much as possible at the office for the past couple days. Ever since their sexually charged moment that ended with her humiliating and hurried exit from her own damn office in order to get her raging hormones in order.

All this time later, and said hormones were *still* rampaging out of control.

But she was working on it. She needed her job way too much to risk screwing it up by sleeping with her boss. No matter how much she wanted to.

And she wanted to—a lot.

Not that this was the time to think about her growing and unhealthy obsession with him.

Did he have to look so freaking good all the time? Today he was the casual host in his white T-shirt and baggy blue board shorts for the pool. This ensemble, of course, highlighted the width of his shoulders, emphasized the muscular cut of his arms and legs, and showcased his gleaming brown skin.

Truly, it wasn't fair.

The man didn't even give women a fighting chance not to fall all over him.

Suddenly Charlotte realized the silence had gone on too long. Giving herself a swift mental kick, she got her head back in the game.

"Thanks for having us," she told him, acutely aware of Mama's pleased smile and sharpened gaze, which was swinging between the two of them. Really, the woman should have just infused Jake's cookies with a love potion and been done with it. Maybe that would satisfy her overactive matchmaking gene. "You have an incredible house."

"Thanks."

More staring between her and Jake ensued.

Mama coughed.

Jake snapped out of it and stepped back, opening the door wider. "Come on in. Hey, buddy. Remember me?"

Harry grinned up at him. "You have fish!"

"That's me. I have fish here, too."

"No way! That's too many fish!"

"You may be right." Jake pointed, though there was no chance of anyone missing the fish tank. "Right over there. Check them out if you want."

To no one's surprise, Harry wanted. Racing through the foyer—what there was of it, since all of the rooms seemed to bleed together—he reached the tank and, true to form, plastered his hands and face up against it.

"Oh, man!" he cried.

Yeah, Charlotte thought. Oh, man. That about covered it.

On the far wall, behind the tufted black leather furniture, was a stunning saltwater aquarium. Actually, no. The aquarium, which had its own interior lights and glowed a brilliant blue, wasn't on the wall. It was built *into* the wall. All kinds of seaweed undulated lazily back and forth, and there was a stunning array of coral and fish, including one with black and tan stripes that looked suspiciously like—

"A shark! Mommy! It's a shark! With teeth!"

Smiling indulgently, clearly thrilled to entertain such a rapt fan of his fish, Jake walked over to stand behind Harry. "It's a bamboo shark, man. He comes from the Pacific Ocean."

"What's his name?"

"His name?" Jake's brow quirked. "You know…I never named him."

"Jake's good with kids," Mama murmured in Charlotte's ear.

Charlotte gave her a sideways glare. "Anyone can be good with kids for thirty seconds once a week, Mama. And why are you commenting?"

"No reason," Mama sang happily.

"You have to name him!" Harry was now informing Jake.

"Yeah, you're probably right," Jake agreed. "What sounds good?"

"Harry's a good name." Harry tilted his head, tugged on his ear and thought hard. "Harry Sharkley!"

Jake's mouth twitched. "Harry Sharkley. Great name. Done."

"Yay!" With that important business out of the way, Harry raced back over to Charlotte and his grandmother. "Grammy! Can we go swimming now? Huh, Grammy? I have my floaty on already! And my trunks!"

The boy had insisted on wearing his Batman trunks and swim vest all morning and while in the car, which had made buckling him into his car seat a challenge, to say the least.

Charlotte's mother, who had the patience of most of the saints when it came to her grandson, gave him an indulgent smile and took his hand to stop him from bouncing like a drunken kangaroo.

"In a minute. Can I say hello to Mr. Hamilton first? Would that be okay with you?"

"No," Harry said, pouting.

She rolled her eyes. "Hello, Jake."

Jake, who'd followed Harry back over, leaned in to give her a peck on the cheek. "Hello, beautiful. Thanks for coming. And are those cookies I see in that container?"

Her mother passed over a giant storage container with approximately three thousand cookies in it. "You haven't tried my sugar cookies yet."

Jake took the container and held it with careful hands, the way he might handle an original of the Declaration of Independence. "God bless you," he said gravely.

"Now wait a minute," her mother said, laughing. "You're supposed to share those with your guests."

"You didn't bring enough for sharing," Jake cried, outraged.

"Mommy!" Harry, who was now at the far end of the living room, in the space between a set of chairs and the granite bar that bordered the gleaming kitchen, started jumping again, gesturing wildly. "Look, Mommy! Toys!"

Toys was an understatement, Charlotte discovered when she wandered over.

The space looked like an FAO Schwarz annex.

There were LEGO blocks, Lincoln Logs and several games, including, she saw at a glance, Sorry, Candy Land, Monopoly and Clue. There were stuffed animals, action figures and—no lie—a Big Wheel. There was even—

"Mommy, look! It's a doll baby, Mommy! A DOLL BABY!"

Harry, who'd apparently found heaven on earth, pulled out a pink-pajama-wearing doll that was half as big as he was and snuggled it to his chest, loving on it. His eyes rolled closed and he swayed, looking like a future father of the year.

"His name is Jeremy," Harry announced.

The adults caught each other's eyes and tried not to snicker.

Charlotte decided that, since she was the mother, it was her job to tackle this tricky subject.

"Ah, Harry," she explained gently. "Usually girl babies wear pink and boy babies—"

Harry stared up at her, the picture of angelic innocence with those big gray eyes. "Mommy, it doesn't matter."

"You're right," Charlotte agreed, feeling that familiar swell of love in her chest for this little darling. "Doesn't matter." She shifted her attention to Jake, who'd been an avid observer of this interchange. "Toys, eh? Did they come with the black leather furniture and sixty-inch TV in this bachelor pad?"

Jake ducked his head, but not before she caught a telltale glimpse of rising color across his cheeks. "Well, you know. Kids need stuff to play with, right? What if they get tired of the pool?"

From out back came the raucous sounds of laughing, shrieking and splashing.

"Good thinking," Charlotte said. "Most kids don't enjoy pools for long."

Jake snorted and dimpled, looking oddly boyish and vulnerable. "You're right. It's too much, isn't it? It's been so long since I was in a toy store, I just got…carried away. It was a lot of fun. You should see the flying helicopter I got myself."

Harry, who'd been kissing Jeremy's cheek, looked up. "FLYING HELICOPTER?"

Charlotte put a restraining arm on his shoulder. "Later for that."

"And I, uh, put those little plastic protectors in all the plugs."

"What?"

"Just in case Harry, you know, runs around trying to stick forks in the plugs or something."

Charlotte's jaw hit the floor. The idea of Jake the Player putting this much effort into their little afternoon visit was overwhelming her brain's electrical circuits.

Jake seemed to be waiting for her approval. "It's way too much, right? You can say it."

What could she say when confronted with such unexpected generosity?

"It is way too much. And incredibly thoughtful. Thank you for thinking of the kids."

Jake stared at her. "Anytime."

"Let's go, little man." Her mother, perhaps sensing a shift in the wind, jumped to life and tugged Harry's hand, leading him toward the glass doors, through which they could see a beautiful deck with several tables covered with red market umbrellas. "Let's go to the pool and see if we can find any kids your age. You folks take your time," she added over her shoulder, giving Charlotte a pointed look. "No rush. I've got things under control."

With that, they disappeared outside, leaving Charlotte alone with Jake.

Neither of them seemed to know what to say to each other.

"So," Jake began. "About that, uh, moment we had the other day…"

There was an apologetic note in his voice, but she didn't need to hear it.

They had chemistry, she and Jake, and they would manage it like the professionals they were.

They had to manage it.

"It's fine," she interjected.

His brow quirked. "Fine?"

"We had a moment, but we're past it now, and it'll never happen again because we're professionals. The end."

Jake's brows had flattened into a thick and forbidding line across his forehead.

"The end," he echoed, low.

"Yes," she said crisply, pivoting on her heel and heading for the deck, which was, with any luck, safer than being alone inside with a Jake who looked like he wanted to either throttle her or swallow her whole. "The end."

And she slipped outside, well aware that this was the second time this week that she'd walked out on Jake, and he was not the sort of man—not at all the sort of man—who'd tolerate her evasions for long.

"Harry Evans Miller," Charlotte called from the edge of the pool, "you come out of there right now. Right. Now."

Harry, who was now flopping around in the kiddy end, making sure to come close enough to taunt her but still stay well out of arm's reach, frowned at her.

"No!" he said snottily.

Charlotte's blood, which had been merely simmering up until now, hit a full rolling boil that was not helped by her audience of amused onlookers. In addition to the other staffers' kids floating nearby, there were her coworkers in the pool and sitting around at the tables, gorging on cookies and cakes and any other food they could get their greedy hands on. There were also her mother, who was hovering at her elbow, eating one of Jake's amazing ribs, and, worst of all, Jake, who'd been horsing around with all the kids, but who now swam over to hook his elbows on the pool's ledge at her feet and watch the unfolding drama.

They'd been out in the hot Indian summer sun for two hours already, and Harry had been in the pool pretty much the entire time, except for a quick five minutes when she'd tempted him out with a hot dog. He'd be nice and tired tonight, which meant he'd sleep well, and that was great.

On the other hand, if he got overtired, which he was in real danger of doing, he'd be a cranky nightmare.

And they really needed to get going because Saturdays were her big days for getting caught up on her schoolwork, and she had tons of reading and studying to do.

Plus, being here at Jake's house was really doing a number on her.

"You want me to grab him and pull him out?" Jake asked, keeping his voice low so that Harry couldn't hear.

Charlotte, who was hot and agitated, fumed. Then she divided her gaze between two things she didn't want to look at: her bratty son, who was now staring her in the face while skimming his arms across the water and getting her feet wet, despite her stern warnings for him to stop doing just that, and Jake, the sexiest man ever to put his board shorts on one leg at a time.

God, he was killing her.

He'd shed his T-shirt hours ago, which meant she'd had plenty of time to ogle him behind the cover of her dark sunglasses. His body was rippled and lean, just muscular enough, with hard bulges in all the right places, which included a butt that formed a perfect half circle. He'd swum a few laps, his long and contoured arms slicing through the water with ridiculous ease, and he'd even demonstrated his butterfly stroke to one of the teenagers and it had been, like everything else about Jake, a thing of beauty.

Now he stared up at her with skin that was a sun-kissed red and water droplets tracing paths down his broad shoulders and torso that she longed to trace with her tongue.

All of which really pissed her off.

With the schoolwork and her out-of-control son, didn't she have enough on her plate at this moment without having to fight her own overactive hormones, as well?

And she couldn't even use her vibrator to take off the edge tonight, unless she made a special stop at the drugstore for batteries.

"No," she snapped at Jake. "Thanks."

"But—"

"He needs to mind when I tell him something," she added, well aware that she'd been rude, and it wasn't Jake's fault that he had her panties in a bunch; he'd just been born that way. "I'll figure this out myself."

Jake didn't look convinced. "But with power struggles—"

She folded her arms across her chest and glared down at him, cutting him off. "I'm sorry. How many children do you have? None, right? So why are you talking?"

Jake threw up his hands and glided back in the water, his eyes aglint with dark amusement. "Okay, then. I'll just keep my unwanted opinions to myself."

"Thank you," Charlotte huffed.

"Honey," her mother whispered in her ear, "why don't I just get a cookie and lure him out with—"

"No. I will handle this."

Shaking her head sadly, Mama also backed off.

"Harry," Charlotte called, holding up three fingers, "this is your final warning. One…two…three."

Harry stuck his tongue out at her.

For one arrested second, a hot red haze of public humiliation blocked her vision and made her face burn to cinders. *Well, shit,* she thought. What the hell was she supposed to do now?

And then she saw a smug two-year-old smile spread across Harry's face.

"Oh, hell, no," she muttered, and jumped, fully clothed, into the pool to get her son.

Charlotte emerged a few seconds later, soaking wet, grim-faced and dignified. Her chin was hitched up, as though she didn't have a squalling and thrashing toddler under her arm, and Jake had never admired her more.

Harry had, in the end, been easy to catch. He'd been so astonished to see his mother dive into the pool that he hadn't scurried away, and that was his fatal mistake. Apparently the boy was as stubborn and proud as she was, because he made quite the humiliated racket.

"I don't wanna go!" And then, in case anyone in the greater Philadelphia area hadn't heard him the first time, "I DON'T WANNA GO!"

Charlotte, ignoring this ongoing protest, hooked him under her arm in a football hold and climbed up the steps, out of the pool.

The adults in the group, apparently recognizing a brilliant act of parenting when they saw it, broke into a round of cheers and applause. The kids, predictably, booed.

Charlotte nodded and raised her free hand in thanks. "I appreciate it, guys."

"Speech! Speech!" someone called.

That cracked her—and everyone else—up.

"Okay," she said finally as Jake climbed out of the pool behind her. "Knock it off."

Mrs. Evans hurried forward and took Harry, whose shrieks were now approaching a piercing frequency that only dogs, bats and dolphins would be able to hear. "I think you've had enough, young man," she told Harry sternly. "I'm taking you to change your clothes. And then we're going to have a long talk about your unacceptable behavior."

Harry hooked his bright red face around his grandmother's shoulder and hiccupped his sobs into submission. "Nooo!" he wailed. "I don't want a talk."

"Then you'd best apologize to Mr. Hamilton," Mrs. Evans snapped, not missing a beat. "Because this isn't a very nice way to act after he invited you to his pool, fed you a delicious lunch, showed you his fish and let you play with Jeremy."

Harry tugged on his ear and raised his head to regard Jake with wet chipmunk cheeks and tragic eyes that were drowning in tears. "Sorry."

Jake's insides melted into a sticky goo along the lines of hot candle wax. "It's okay, buddy. It's been a long day."

"Can I still hold Jeremy?" Harry asked, his lower lip trembling with misery.

Jake opened his mouth, about to tell Harry that he could have Jeremy, all the toys inside the house, and all the cookies and hot dogs he could eat, if only he'd stop crying and tearing him up inside, but Charlotte, apparently fearing something along those lines, cleared her throat.

"We'll see about Jeremy," she told Harry, now examining towels on the nearest lounger. "Maybe if you behave while Grammy gets your clothes back on, you can hold Jeremy again before we leave. But we are leaving. Okay?"

Harry, the picture of toddler heartbreak, dropped his head back onto Mrs. Evans's shoulder, nodded, popped his thumb in his mouth and held Jake's gaze as Mrs. Evans snatched up the diaper bag and headed into the house.

Jake watched them go, quite certain that he'd just lost a big chunk of his heart to a kid that wasn't even his.

"I'm really sorry," Charlotte said quietly.

Jake glanced back around. "Huh? Sorry? For what? Having a normal kid?"

"Disrupting your nice picnic. Poor kid control. Wearing clothes in your pool. Pick one."

"Well, now you raise an interesting point. Because most people wore a bathing suit."

"I didn't want to get my hair wet," she said glumly, reaching up to wring said hair and splattering water onto the deck. "You don't have a towel I can borrow, do you? These are all wet."

"Yeah. Come on."

He started to lead her inside, but she checked herself at the glass door. "What?"

"I don't want to drip on your nice floors."

He snorted. Like he cared about a little water. "You women are strange creatures. I'm dripping, too, in case you hadn't noticed. Let's go."

They headed inside and down the hallway, with Charlotte's shoes squelching behind him, and paused while he checked the linen closet. No towels; he'd grabbed all of them earlier and left them poolside for the guests.

"I have some in my bathroom," he told her. "Just did the laundry."

"Good. And may I congratulate you on your superlative climate control?"

The air-conditioning, he realized, was making her shiver. "I like to keep it cool around here. In case any polar bears drop by."

"They'll feel right at home."

From the powder room at the other end of the house came the distant sounds of Harry whining and Mrs. Evans scolding. Charlotte paused, glancing over her shoulder.

"God bless Mama," she said fervently.

"How do you do it?" he asked her.

"What?"

"Discipline Harry when he needs it. Those big teary eyes were killing me."

"Wake up," she commanded, snapping her fingers right in front of his face. "If you show weakness to a toddler—" she slashed her hand across her neck "—it's over for you, man. He'd eat you for a snack along with his Goldfish and animal crackers."

Their mutual laughter trailed off and died as they turned into his spacious bedroom.

He had no idea what she was thinking.

All he could think about was how much he'd love to have her, naked, sweat-slicked and panting, in his king-size bed.

"You're neat," she noted, looking around the room.

"True."

He made up the mahogany four-poster first thing every morning, and the nightstands, leather chairs and benches were, he figured, too nice for him to use as dirty clothes racks. He had matching taupe curtains, duvet and pillows, and the sisal rug kept the hardwood floor from being too cold for his tootsies if he used the bathroom in the night.

"You have a beautiful house," she told him.

He knew that, of course, having worked really hard to earn the house. All of his guests, as they had arrived today for the barbecue, had told him how great his house was.

So why did Charlotte's compliment, above all others, make him this unreasonably happy?

He cleared his throat and tried to tame his grin. "Thanks."

He gestured to the bathroom door, but Charlotte had

paused to check his nightstand reading. Her lips curled into a bemused smile.

"Jacques Cousteau, eh?"

"Well, you know," he said, distracted both by her proximity to the bed and the way her filmy wet dress clung to her toned legs and round ass. He noticed she was wearing black bikini panties. "I like fish and all."

"And Jules Verne."

She picked up the leather-bound volume and turned to face him, flipping through it.

Ah, shit. Now that she'd dropped her arms, he saw the way her dress and bra had gone sheer. Her breasts— two big ovals with pointed nipples the color and shape of Hershey's Kisses chocolates—were on prominent and breathtaking display.

And she evidently had no idea.

"Twenty Thousand Leagues Under the Sea," she said brightly.

His mouth was dry, his tongue thick. "What else?"

The thing he needed to do, he decided with the only bit of his brain that was still functioning properly—a tiny little back corner that was grinding along at about 10 percent, maybe less—was stop staring, find her a damn towel and get her, and her adorable family, out of his house as soon as possible.

Yes.

Because he was trying to do the honorable thing for once in his life, which was nothing less than Charlotte deserved.

The honorable thing. Which did not, he was pretty

sure, include tossing Charlotte onto his bed and ravishing her for a week or two.

So he hurried into his Italian-tiled bathroom, clicked on the light and reached for the shelf that held his thick white bath sheets. He'd just grabbed one, shaken it out and turned back to the door, when Charlotte arrived and caught a glance of herself in the huge mirror.

She went beet red and crossed her hands over her breasts.

"Oh, my God," she gasped.

Something came over him in the superheated silence that followed as their gazes met and locked.

Maybe it was her embarrassment when, as far as he was concerned, her being nude or nearly so, here, with him, was the most natural and inevitable thing in the world.

Maybe it was exhaustion at fighting what would ultimately be a losing battle at keeping his hands to himself.

Maybe it was, simply, the realization that he was a strong man who could control a lot of things in his life, but his growing feelings for Charlotte Evans would never fall into that category.

Drifting closer, he stared at her, taking into account her dripping hair, water-streaked makeup and brilliant gray eyes.

"You don't know how beautiful you are," he softly told her. "You don't know how much I think about you."

"Jake." His name was a whisper. A sigh. A promise. She tipped up her chin and watched him with glittering eyes that were already half closed, surrendering even as she continued to fight. "I thought we agreed we weren't going to do this."

Reaching up, mesmerized by everything about this one special woman, he smoothed the wet hair past her temple. Traced one silky brow. Ran his thumb across the dewy velvet of her lower lip.

"I've been trying." He shrugged helplessly. "I didn't know how hard it would be."

Leaning in, he dipped his head and, making sure to keep their bodies well apart, kissed her before she could protest—one gentle, lingering, perfect kiss that nearly choked him with desire.

Then he pulled back, knowing he'd crossed a line but unable to remember why that should matter.

Her eyes were bright and glazed now, a vivid mixture of gray and green that should only belong to the finest jewels and sunset-streaked oceans.

"You're so beautiful," he said again, shaking his head because life was unfair. Why else would God drop this woman in his life and then make her off-limits? "So beautiful."

"So are you."

With that sweet murmur, she stepped forward, into his impatient arms, and slid her hands across his shoulders to his neck, bringing him down to her with an urgency that almost matched his own. Their bodies sealed together of their own accord, and the yielding pressure of her sex against him brought him to a full and raging erection.

With this second kiss, all bets were off.

Her breathy mewl set something loose inside him, and he responded with a strange sound that was throaty and animalistic. Planting his hands in her wet hair, reaching for the warm scalp beneath, he angled her head to deepen the kiss. She opened for him, her tongue meeting his thrust for thrust, and her mouth was honey fresh…hot…greedy.

Escalating the situation was the worst possible idea, but he couldn't stop himself from running his fingers down her supple back, to her ass. He filled his hands with her, circling his hips in a thrust that—

"Mommy? MOMMY!"

Harry's voice was, thankfully, still distant, but it worked with the violent efficiency of a nuclear strike. They jumped apart, stiffening, and she rubbed her lips and then her face.

Jake, meanwhile, trembled with the effort to control his frustrated need. "Charlotte—"

The horrified regret in her eyes was like a jabbing stab wound as she pointed her finger in his face. "Don't. I need my job, so we're not doing this. Even if we want to."

She hurried out, wrapping the towel up under her arms and around her torso as she went.

He rested his palms on the unyielding granite counter, willing his body to cool down.

By the time he emerged from the bedroom a couple minutes later, Charlotte, Harry and Mrs. Evans were gathered in the foyer, ready to go. Mrs. Evans and Harry had changed into dry clothes, and Harry, who still had his thumb in his mouth, was drowsy-eyed in his little jeans shorts and striped T-shirt.

Jake tried to play the gracious host, but it was hard when his lust and emotional turmoil had him tied up in knots. Since he didn't trust himself to look at Charlotte just yet, and Mrs. Evans had a speculative glint in her eyes that made him wonder if she doubled as a detective for the police department, he stooped down and focused his goodbye on Harry.

"Thanks for coming, little man."

"Thanks for having me," Harry said glumly.

"What's wrong?"

"I want to stay here."

"Oh," Jake said, blindsided by this little bit of news and by how much he'd miss this little guy when he left. "Well." He glanced up at Charlotte, who was pointedly looking in the other direction, at the fish tank. "Maybe you can come back sometime. If you listen to your mom. Okay?"

Harry nodded. "Can I say goodbye to Jeremy?"

"Yeah. Of course you can." Jake glanced around for the doll but Mrs. Evans produced it from behind her back and handed it to Jake. "Thanks. Here you go, Harry."

Harry grinned with delight around his thumb and hugged the doll to his chest.

And then, to Jake's utter astonishment, he threw his little arms around Jake and hugged him, too.

Some primal paternal instinct blossomed into action for the first time ever, and Jake found himself sweeping Harry up into a bear hug that probably should have crushed his tiny bones.

He stood, swaying and enjoying the way Harry clung to him with surprising strength.

How long should a hug like that last?

Was an hour too long?

Jake turned his head and kissed Harry on the cheek, intending to put him down before he decided to keep him, but then he noticed something.

"Charlotte," he said, "should Harry feel this warm?"

"Oh, great." Charlotte exchanged a dark look with her mother, then leaned in to press her lips to Harry's forehead. "Harry! You have a fever, buddy. How does your ear feel?"

"Hurts," Harry said drowsily.

"Well, why didn't you mention it?"

"I wanted to swim."

Smart kid.

"I noticed he felt warm," Mrs. Evans admitted. "But I thought it was from the sun and the tantrum."

Jake tried not to overreact, but he was definitely concerned. They had this under control, right?

"So, what happens now?" he asked. "Antibiotics or something?"

"Yeah," said Charlotte tiredly. "We'll have to run him by urgent care since it's after hours on Saturday. Again. He's prone to ear infections."

"Oh." Jake remembered what she kept telling him about the complexity of her life. "And you have studying to do tonight, right? How will you—"

Charlotte took Harry from him and settled him against her own shoulder. Despite the little guy's sturdy weight, her back was strong and there was no self-pity in her expression—just a wry smile.

"Mothers manage," she said simply.

"Jake?" Harry asked.

Jake peeled away his gaze from the incredible woman in front of him and focused on her son. "Yep?"

"Can I borrow Jeremy? Till I get my ear fixed?"

Jake was too moved to speak.

"Please?" Harry added.

Jake swallowed hard, trying to dislodge a lump the size of his heart from his tight throat. "Yeah. Sure."

Jake's gaze was irrevocably drawn back to Charlotte, whose color was still high after their interlude in the bathroom. Did she know that he'd lied about the toys being for the kids? That he'd raided the toy store and childproofed his house because he'd wanted to demonstrate that he was a responsible adult who could do a good job with her kid? That the toys for older kids had been a mere afterthought following picking out everything he'd thought Harry would enjoy? Did she have any idea that he'd staked out his front door and ignored all his other guests this afternoon, basically living and breathing for Charlotte's arrival? Did she know his lips still tingled from the sweet pressure of her kiss?

Was this what it was like to fall in love? He almost wished he could ask her, because God knew he had no experience in this terrifying area.

Tearing away his attention from Charlotte, he handed the doll to Harry.

He had the terrifying thought, as he did so, that he'd also handed his heart over to this family—to Charlotte—without even realizing it.

Chapter 9

"Thanks for letting me come," Roger said early that evening.

"Thanks for calling first this time."

Charlotte shut her apartment door behind him and trailed him into the dimly lit living room, where Harry was lying on the sofa beneath a plush blue blanket. Fast asleep, he had his curly head—and Jeremy's—resting on a pillow. The TV had been playing the Disney Channel, but now that Roger was here, she clicked it off and slumped into the nearest cozy chair.

Roger sat on the coffee table facing Harry and watched him with tired eyes. As usual, he was coming off a shift—or going back on to a shift; she no longer bothered keeping his schedule straight—and had that hollowed-out look of utter exhaustion.

Which meant that he looked exactly the way she felt.

After the long wait at urgent care and the trip to the pharmacy for meds, she'd brought Harry home, tried to feed him dinner, bathed him and settled him onto the sofa for TV, battling his illness-induced crankiness all the way.

Homework? She'd never gotten further than opening her books and spreading them on the kitchen table. Reading? It was hard to read when her bleary eyes kept blurring or rolling closed. Sleep? Probably not possible tonight.

She was still too wired from kissing Jake.

"How's he doing?" Roger murmured.

"I think he's more comfortable now that the meds kicked in. He'll feel better tomorrow, after a good night's sleep."

"Did you dose him for the fever?"

"Yeah. And my mom is taking him for the night so she can spoil him to death and I can get some homework done. She'll be here in a minute."

She'd be surprised if he kicked up a fuss about not being offered the first option to take Harry if she needed the night off, and she was right. Roger valued his me-time way too much for that sort of thing, and anyway, his attention had snagged on the doll.

He pointed. "What's this?"

"A doll," she said, too dull-witted by this point to see where the conversation was headed.

Roger turned to her, a frown creasing his forehead. He put a protective hand on Harry's back. "You bought him a doll?"

Uh-oh.

"No," she said slowly, giving him a pointed look. "We went to a work barbecue this afternoon. He got it there. Why?"

"I don't want my son playing with dolls. For obvious reasons."

There was an insinuation about boys, dolls and sexuality in there somewhere, and she nailed him with a cold stare because she didn't want to hear it. "I don't think your reasons are obvious at all. Harry can play with a doll if he wants to. Who cares? Big deal."

Roger had the decency to flush and drop his aggressive stare, but he wasn't finished with the questioning. "A work thing, eh? Where at?"

Double *uh-oh.*

"Jake's," she admitted.

The neutral tone didn't fool Roger, whose shoulders squared off and brows flattened. "And who at the work thing gave him the doll?"

She hesitated, knowing she was about to throw a big scoop of lard right on the fire. But lying wasn't an option; all he had to do was ask Harry the same question, and he'd learn the truth.

"Jake."

His lips twisted into an *ain't-that-some-shit* sneer. "He wants you. You know that, right?"

Again, why lie? "Yes."

"So, you put him in his place, right?"

Charlotte opened her mouth. She wanted to say that, a) it was none of Roger's business; and, moreover, b) she was more than smart enough not to get involved with her boss.

After several long beats, the terrible truth occurred to her: while it may not be Roger's business, she wasn't as smart as she'd hoped she was. Because she wanted Jake and, worse than that, she thought about him. Admired him. Respected him.

Cared for him.

Her face in flames, she shut her mouth and turned away from the stunned realization on Roger's face.

"So it's like that," he said.

Again, she couldn't answer.

The moment's significance was heavy and overwhelming. She and Roger had had their ups, downs, breakups and reconciliations, and she'd had a date with someone else here or there, but there'd never been another significant man. Never been a serious rival for her affections.

Now, it seemed, there was.

Whether she liked it or not, she would have to deal with Jake.

One other thing had changed between her and Roger. Looking at him now, seeing his hurt and jealousy, she felt…nothing. Not joy or triumph, not anger, bitterness or hope for a new and better beginning for their little family.

Just…nothing.

As long as Roger was a good father to their son, she didn't care what he did, or with whom. Maybe, with time, they'd come to be dear friends, but for now there was only neutrality, and that was a huge relief from their emotional roller coaster.

Something in her expression tipped him off.

Nostrils flaring, he swallowed hard, looking vulnerable and boyish—more like the college boy she'd loved than the man he was still becoming.

"It's really over, isn't it?"

"Yes," she said softly.

The pain of this admission carved deep grooves in his face.

"You don't love me anymore, do you?"

That sounded harsher than she was prepared to be. "I'll always—"

"Do you?"

Since he seemed to need the unvarnished truth, she gave it to him. "No."

He swiped at his eyes, got up and headed for the front door. She followed, propelled by the feather lightness of this new freedom from her past and their tangled relationship. This was the first time she'd known, on a cellular level, that she and Roger were forever finished, and the idea thrilled her as much as it terrified her.

Roger, on the other hand, looked crushed. Pausing on the threshold, he turned to issue a bravado-laced warning.

"Harry's only ever going to have one daddy. You know that, right?"

Images flashed through her mind's eye: Jake and Harry bonding over a shared love of fish and cookies; Jake and Harry splashing together in the pool; Jake gifting Harry with a doll and making sure his house was safe for a curious toddler.

And then, too late, she caught herself and slammed the lid on her foolish daydreams.

Maybe she was a smitten fool, but even in her bewitched state, she knew that confirmed players like Jake Hamilton would never make good bonus daddies.

The knowledge hurt, and yet...

"Harry will only ever have one daddy, yeah. But one day, if he's lucky, he'll have another man who loves him like his own," she said quietly, shutting the door in Roger's face.

By nine-thirty, Charlotte had finished her homework, which proved how amazingly efficient she could be when Harry wasn't derailing her train of thought every fifteen seconds. At loose ends, but still feeling relieved after her conversation with Roger, she showered and threw on her silky pink robe over her panties while a load of clothes that included her camis and shorts ran through the dryer.

She was just turning off a couple of the lamps, picking up the TV remote and considering the relative merits of mindlessly flipping channels versus putting in a DVD, when her phone rang. Her first thought was that Harry had taken a turn for the worse and needed to come home, but a quick glance at the display showed that it was the doorman downstairs.

"Is that you, Arnie?" she asked. "What's up?"

"Hey, Charlotte. I've got a delivery for you. A Jake Hamilton—"

Jake?

"—dropped off a couple bags of what looks like groceries. Do you want to come down or should I bring them up for you?"

Groceries? Why on earth would Jake bring her *groceries?* As that tidbit registered with her brain, it was suddenly overrun with other thoughts: *Jake. Here.*

"Is he gone?" she asked.

"Just leaving through the revolving door," said Arnie.

A wild recklessness came over her. "Can you catch him and send him up, please?"

"You got it."

She hung up, her heart rate galloping into triple digits, probably because she knew she was about to do something she'd regret—and regret sooner, rather than later. But Jake was here, and she was alone for the night, and what were the chances of the stars aligning like that on the very day that Jake had kissed her senseless?

If she went into this with eyes wide open and no expectations, then the situation could be managed, couldn't it? Couldn't she take a break from her duties as mother, daughter, student and paralegal and steal this one moment out of time for herself?

One night with Jake before she returned to her responsibilities and he returned to the string of women he kept on retainer. They were consenting adults, weren't they? Where was the harm?

All of her rationalizations were nonsense, she knew. The situation—an affair with her boss—was so dangerous that it should probably be stamped with a giant skull and crossbones as a warning to the foolhardy and self-destructive, which she clearly was.

But as she heard Jake's soft tap on her front door, she didn't care.

Couldn't make herself care.

She opened the door. Her mouth was dry and her blood was hot. "Hey."

"Hey," Jake said.

Now wearing a T-shirt and shorts, he had a couple brown paper bags hugged to his chest and shadows under his eyes. There was a furrow in his brow, as though he didn't know what to make of being invited up to her apartment, and he hovered halfway in and halfway out, unsure.

"I didn't mean to disturb you," he told her.

"You didn't."

"How's Harry?"

"He's okay. I think he feels much better now that we've given him antibiotics and something for the fever. He's spending the night with my mother."

"Oh," Jake said faintly.

He'd noticed her significant lack of clothing, which was no surprise since his blood was redder than that of most other men she knew. His gaze skimmed her up and down, noting, she was sure, the way she'd loosely belted her silk robe, allowing it to pull apart as the edges dipped between her braless breasts, her plump thighs and her bare legs.

She stilled, letting him look.

He blinked and caught himself. His gaze, dark and turbulent now, flicked back to hers.

He didn't speak.

"What're you doing here?"

A rough swallow made his Adam's apple bob. "I, uh…after everyone left, I went online and did some research about kids and ears. Maybe a little too much research, because I wound up scaring myself. Did you know some infections can lead to ruptures and hearing loss?"

She opened her mouth. He didn't give her a chance to answer.

"So, anyway, then I realized I was freaking myself out and decided to do something helpful instead. So I, uh—" his gaze dropped to her cleavage and darted back up again "—I, uh, went to the store and bought you some supplies."

"Supplies?"

"Yeah." He peeked inside the bags, reminding himself. "Tylenol, right, but if he's allergic to Tylenol or something, I got Advil. And then they've got all these flavors, like bubblegum and cherry, so I got him one of each, because I didn't know what flavor he likes."

"You did all that?"

"Plus, while I was in the pharmacy area, I picked up a thermometer, just in case yours was, you know, broken or something. Then I figured sick kids like Popsicles, so I got him some of those. In, uh, multiple flavors."

"No way," she said, grinning now.

"At the checkout line, I started thinking about how bored you might be, cooped up with a sick kid, so I got you some magazines. News and, uh, fashion. Oh, and a couple tabloids, so you'll be up on all the celebrity gossip."

"You're unbelievable."

"And I brought you a bunch of, uh, desserts from the picnic, since I know you like them and I didn't think you got the chance to eat any."

"Is that it?"

Jake cocked his head and thought hard. "Yeah. That about covers it."

"Thank you."

The heartfelt appreciation seemed to embarrass him. Flushing, he ducked his head. "It's nothing. I hope it helps a little. You've got so much on your plate."

A little chip of ice embedded itself in her heart because she didn't like the sound of that. "So that's why you're here, then? I'm a helpless charity case?"

Something new—admiration?—began to gleam in his eyes. "You're many things, Charlotte," he said, unsmiling, "but a helpless charity case isn't one of them."

"I don't like pity," she warned.

"Good, because I'm not offering any."

With that important issue resolved, she nodded and pointed to the kitchen table. "Can you put the bags there, please?"

"Yeah." He strode inside and set down the groceries. "And then I'll get out of your way. I was going to call first, but I figured you'd tell me not to come and I— Ah, shit."

She'd come up behind him, pressing her body along the length of his and reaching under his T-shirt to skim her hands across the taut skin of his belly. All of his muscles tightened beneath his satin flesh, and a shudder rippled through him along with a low groan.

"Stay with me," she murmured, rubbing her aching breasts against his back and gliding her hands up his torso so she could ease the shirt off over his head. "I want you."

Things did not go as planned.

Instead of sweeping her up into his arms or down onto the floor, he wrenched free, pulling down his shirt, wheeled around and grabbed her by the upper arms, ignoring her shocked cry. Giving her a little jerk, he stooped just enough to stare her in the eyes and nail her with a hot fury that looked like it had been building for years.

"Is this a game to you?" he demanded.

"What? No!"

"This afternoon you tell me this isn't going to happen, and now *this?* Why the turnaround, Charlotte? You like playing with my head? Is that it?"

Setting her arms free, he yanked her robe's belt loose and pulled the edges apart. This time, there was nothing discreet about his gaze. It was fierce and unabashed, taking in everything from her jutting nipples to the scrap of white lace that passed as her underwear.

"Do you know how much I've wanted you—just like this?" Reaching out, he cupped her breasts, filling his gentle hands with her and rubbing his thumbs in rhythmic circles around her aureoles until her breath came in great, heaving strains. "And now you're taunting me with this body? Do you get a thrill driving me out of my freaking mind? Huh?"

"No."

"Then why are you doing this?"

"I told you already." Forcing her slumberous eyes all the way open, she held his inflamed gaze so he'd see that she didn't have any ulterior motives. "I want you."

His expression shifted, softening into a wild hope that filled her up inside and threatened to overflow. Without warning, he took her face in his hands and angled her head way back. The kiss was hard and deep, so urgent that the sweet pain of his nips only magnified her pleasure a millionfold.

She panted and mewled, uninhibited in a way she'd never thought was possible, and this time he raised his arms to help her get his T-shirt up and off. Dropping it to the floor, she planted her hands where she wanted them, on the unyielding slabs of his chest, and just touched him, smoothing and stroking, scratching and swirling.

He went wild.

Shuddering with restraint and muttering curses interspersed with praise about her breasts and her skin, her eyes and her mouth, he clamped his hands on her butt and hefted her. She helped, wrapping her legs around his waist and her arms around his neck as he swung her around and set her on the hard edge of the oak kitchen table. When his hands went to the edges of the robe, she relaxed her shoulders and let the silk slither to the floor.

Gripping the wide span of her hips to hold her in place, he stared at her with eyes so hot she might have been pressed up against the sun. A sudden impulsive euphoria made her smile as she kissed him and went to work on his belt, and his white smile flashed back at her before he bent at the waist to pull his wallet and cell phone out of a pocket and kick off his shorts and underwear.

Then he tossed his cell phone on the counter and straightened and stood there, between her thighs. The sight of him emptied all the air out of her straining lungs.

His skin gleamed, warm and brown, in the dim lighting. A fine streak of hair ran between his flat dark nipples, tapering through the rungs of his abdomen and flaring again as it reached his groin. His erection was thick and insistent, and she reached for him, wrapping his length in a firm grip that made his breath hiss and his eyes roll closed.

He'd been reaching in his wallet to pull out a foil package, but now he caught her wrist, stopping her.

"What?" she whispered, the lust making her impatient. It felt like she'd waited for this moment, with him, for all of her life, and she didn't want to stop now. Was he deciding she wasn't worth the effort or risk to his career? Did he have second thoughts already? "What is it?"

His eyes opened, and they were as feverish as Harry's had been earlier. "This isn't a game," he told her again, a clear note of warning in his voice.

"I know." She watched as he ripped open the package with his teeth and sheathed himself. And then, because he didn't look convinced, she said it again. "I know, Jake."

This was a lie. In that supercharged moment, all she cared about was Jake sliding inside her body and filling her up the way she'd always wished he would. She had no idea what he was getting at. All she knew was that he affected her more than any man ever had, and she needed him now.

"I don't think you do know," he said grimly. His long fingers slid between her legs and found the place where she was swollen and wet for him, engorged with a sweet ache that made her want to squirm out of her skin. "You don't have any idea how I feel about you, do you?"

"Jake—"

"I think I'm falling in love with you."

Before the shock of that statement could fully register, he'd taken his length in hand and eased inside her, one exquisite inch at a time. The knife's edge she'd been teetering on shifted, and she dissolved into waves of ecstasy even before he found his rhythm and began to move inside her.

Chapter 10

Jake lay on his side and smoothed Charlotte's thick black hair away from her face as she drowsed, fully aware that he'd lost his mind and lapsed into flaming insanity. They were stretched out on the bed in her dark bedroom now, their limbs twined and still slick with sweat. Too wired to sleep, he'd propped himself on one elbow and adjusted the wooden blinds behind the headboard to allow the full moon's light to filter in.

He wanted to see her features better while he traced them with the fingers of his free hand.

Crazy, right?

Who knew he had this sticky core of sappiness running down his spine?

She was amazing, his Charlotte, and everything

about her fascinated him. Her arched brows were silky, but her forehead was velvety. Her nose tipped up just a bit at the end, giving it a perky look that he loved, and her mouth…

Man, he loved that mouth.

Her plump lips were dewy and slightly parted, still swollen from his kisses, and just looking at that delicious mouth got him fired up again even though his body continued to vibrate with satisfaction and triumph. Was he supposed to feel as though he'd won the lottery because Charlotte made love with him? Was that normal?

He had no way of knowing since he'd never felt like this—or anything close to this—before.

Hell. A great white shark knew more about flying an airplane than he knew about being in love.

But he was. He wasn't sure how it had happened, or why it had happened with such dizzying speed, but he was.

He hadn't meant to tell her, though. It was too much, too soon. They were just getting to know each other, and the last thing he wanted to do was scare her away, which seemed like a real possibility given her personal history.

Plus, he'd had no idea he was even capable of spelling the word *love,* much less confessing it. The closest he'd come in previous relationships was telling a woman that he *liked* the way her butt looked in some jeans or would *like* to sleep with her.

Love?

He hadn't seen that coming.

The question loomed before him: *What now, genius?*

They'd have to give that a lot of thought and discussion, wouldn't they?

For now, though, her mouth needed some attention.

Leaning in, he gave her a lingering nuzzle, followed by a kiss and a nip, and she stirred, curling those lips into a sleepy and satisfied smile that made renewed desire pool, low and heavy, in his groin.

Her lids flickered open. "Hi," she said, her voice husky and unbearably sexy.

Sudden fear tightened his throat, making it hard for him to speak. This was way too soon, he knew, and it mattered way too much to him. Making love with Charlotte this early in their fledgling relationship would, one way or another, come back to bite him in the ass, not that he'd take it back or anything. He wanted Charlotte with an urgency that damn near embarrassed him, and he'd take her any way he could have her, soon or otherwise. In fact, he was surprised he'd played the gentleman for this long and was rather proud of himself for doing so.

God knew he'd never been known for having a noble streak.

But there'd be a price to pay for becoming intimate this quickly, because they hadn't settled anything about their relationship, and that was just how life worked.

"Hi," he said.

She stretched a little, arching into him, and his mind was already scrolling ahead, thinking about how freaking perfect it was to be here with her now and wondering how he was supposed to be happy in a bed without her from now on. Because she was the type of mother who'd protect her child from any new boyfriends she had until she knew the man was a keeper, and she hadn't given him that seal of approval yet. Which, of course, meant that he wouldn't be rolling around in any beds with Charlotte on the nights Harry was with her—most nights, that was.

Yeah, he thought sourly, missing her already.

He was screwed every way he looked at it.

"What's wrong?"

Staring into that amazing face with her nude and supple body wrapped around his?

"Not a damn thing," he assured her.

"How'd we make it to the bed?" she wondered, shifting to her side to face him.

"I have no present recollection of that event," he told her in his best courtroom voice. "I wasn't in my right mind."

They grinned at each other, and he found himself loving her a little bit harder.

"You have a great apartment."

"Yeah?" she asked, running her thumb over his lips as he spoke.

"Yeah."

What he didn't mention was that the reason it was great was because it was as warm and welcoming as his house was cool and sterile. Her leather furniture, he'd seen at a glance, was weathered and looked comfortable, as though it was for using rather than looking at. His leather furniture, meanwhile, was like a work of art to be admired but not employed.

She had pillows, bookshelves and candles burning, not because she'd been planning some big seduction scene, but just because she apparently liked their floral scent. His house smelled like…empty. Lonely. Best of all, her bed was big, fluffy, warm and covered with mountains of soft pillows, which made for interesting possibilities for lovemaking positions. His bed was… big.

"I really like it here. I hope I'll be hanging around a lot."

That was her cue to lob some welcoming comment back at him. Something like *Oh, Jake, I want you here with me all the time!* But she didn't. Instead, she blinked a couple times, her pleased expression clouding over and then, right out of the blue, she hit him with a toughie.

"Why me, Jake?"

Funny she should ask, he thought, losing himself in her eyes, which were intent and vulnerable.

He'd spent a lot of time asking himself variations of that same question that went a little something like this: why—and how—had this one female captured his attention and interest so completely?

The world was full of women, which was great for him because he enjoyed women and had enjoyed more than his fair share of them. That being the case, why had Charlotte become the sole woman in vivid HD and 3-D brilliance, when all the other women he'd been involved with were like black-and-white magazine photos?

Yeah, the difference between Charlotte and every-one else was *that* glaring.

"Let's see." He chose his words carefully, trying to identify what made her so special and wanting to get this right so she'd never wonder again. "You're smart and beautiful. You're funny and sweet. You're strong, determined, driven and a great mother. You're crazy sexy. Hang on…am I missing anything?"

"Jake—"

"Shh. You think too much. You worry too much." He tapped his index finger against her lips so she wouldn't protest as she clearly wanted to. Dipping his head, he kissed her again, right between the eyes, where her brow was furrowed with thought. "I don't think the question is *Why you?* I think the question is *Who else?*"

Behind his finger, her lips curled in the beginnings of a smile. "That's the problem with being involved with a lawyer. You have an argument for everything, don't you?"

"It's not an argument. It's how I feel."

Something about his earnestness seemed to unset-tle her, because that cloud drifted in again, shadowing her face. "This is insane. I don't know what we think we're doing."

Yeah. Neither did he.

But now wasn't the time to begin those discussions. Now was the time to learn the feel of her body—which his fingers set out to do—and what she liked and what made her—

"Jake!"

His name was a sharp cry of pleasure, and he loved the way it sounded. So he trailed his fingers lower across her belly, just grazing the place where smooth skin gave way to coarse curls, and smiled at the way she cooed and dissolved against him.

"Right now?" He gave the sheet a tug, pulling it down until she was spread out before him—paradise on a bed, and all his to enjoy. Which made him a lucky bastard. "We're going to make love again."

"I don't know." She pouted, scraping her nails up his back as he eased on top of her and settled between her thighs. "I'm not really in the mood. Sorry."

"No need to apologize." He ran his tongue down the tender column of her neck, flicked it over each of her nipples and dipped it into her belly button, which made her giggle and writhe. Then he took firm hold of her hips and shifted into position, lowering his head. "I plan to change your mind."

Charlotte leaned against the back of her armchair for balance as she struggled into her Capri pants and shirt, tasks that would be easier if her hands weren't shaking so badly. Plus, in her panic, she hadn't bothered to turn on any lights, and dawn's weak sunlight filtering through the blinds wasn't enough to penetrate the gloom. She'd be lucky if her clothes even matched, not that she cared at the moment. Swiping a brush through her hair, she hurried to the bed.

Jake lay there, sprawled on his belly with the comforter riding low over his perfectly round butt. Looking at him was a pleasure she'd probably never get used to, even now, when she was quite sure she hated him. His skin gleamed, warmly brown, and his face was utterly relaxed in sleep, giving her a glimpse of the angelic boy he must've been once.

Too bad that boys became men.

"Jake," she said sharply. "Wake up."

He jumped, levering up on his elbows and looking at her with drowsy eyes. "What's wrong?" The sound of his husky early-morning voice was incredibly sexy, and she considered it a sign of her idiocy where he was concerned that she'd notice at a time like this. "Did I oversleep?"

"No." Picking up his cell phone, which she'd set on the nightstand while she dressed, she lobbed it at him harder than she'd meant to—or maybe not—and it barely missed nailing him in the nose. "Here's your phone."

"Hey!"

"You have a text," she informed him, turning away to find some sandals so she didn't have to look into his bewildered face at this galling moment. "I didn't mean to see it, but it was on the kitchen counter and it buzzed when I was in there."

There was a quick silence during which he read the text—or was *sext* the appropriate term?—which was forever scorched across her poor brain:

Hey JJ—
I'll be in town over the weekend.

Can you take me around the world again?
No one makes me scream like you do.
CC
XXOXOX

She and CC would probably never meet, Charlotte thought bitterly, but they had something in common, didn't they? They'd both benefitted from Jake's prodigious bedroom skills.

Jake cursed. The next thing she knew, he was standing next to her, a sheet tied around his narrow waist and a whole lot of *let-me-explain* in his eyes.

"CC's a classmate of mine from law school. We've hooked up here and there when she's in town. It was never anything other than sex. I'm going to text her back and tell her I'm involved with someone, and then I'll probably never see her again."

Though she'd desperately hoped he'd have just such an explanation, hearing it only infuriated her more. Because here was proof—more proof, actually—that Jake went through women the way Starbucks went through coffee beans. So he decided he was finished with a woman? No problem. He'd just send her a text and be done with her.

She stared at him and worked hard to manage both her temper and her grief. Because here, already, was irrefutable evidence that things between her and Jake were not sustainable and would inevitably end badly. She felt like she'd lost something enormous, and wasn't that stupid? How could you lose what you'd never had to begin with?

"Why would you bother?" she wondered. "See her again if you want. It has nothing to do with me, *JJ.*"

This pronouncement didn't sit well with him, and his brows lowered accordingly, as did his voice. "Excuse me?"

"In the light of day, I think you'll agree that sleeping with your employee was a colossal mistake that we shouldn't repeat—"

"I *don't* agree—"

"—and you are therefore free to sleep with your law school classmate, or the barista at Starbucks who was making eyes at you, or the woman who called and wanted to cook you dinner, or any other woman who's willing to take you on. That should make you happy."

"It won't."

"In fact, maybe the best thing is for me to quit."

"*Quit?* That's insane."

"No. Insane is sleeping with my boss, the player, and thinking it won't lead to disaster."

"Charlotte." A flare of panic seemed to hit him, making his eyes flash. He reached for her upper arm and held it in his firm grip. "Some other woman can't make me happy. I thought we established that last night. Making love isn't a disaster. It's the best thing that's—"

She jerked free. She didn't need his hot touch any more than she needed reminders of what he'd said last night and what she'd almost allowed herself to believe. "I don't have time for this—"

"Don't have time?"

"The reason I was in the kitchen earlier when you got your little text is because my mother's neighbor called." That stifling fear swelled inside her again, and she had to force a deep breath or risk a full-blown panic attack. "Mama's having chest pains and they had to take her to the hospital."

"What?"

"Which means I need to pick up Harry, who must be scared to death because he doesn't know the neighbor. I need to get him to Roger's and then get to the hospital, hopefully before my mother goes into surgery or cardiac arrest." Growing hysteria made her voice shrill at the end, and she took another breath. "So you need to get dressed and leave."

"I'll come to the hospital with you," he said quickly. "I don't want you to be alone waiting for news."

"No, thanks. I'll be fine."

"You won't be fine," he said, incredulous. "No one is fine by themselves in a hospital waiting room. You'll need someone there with you."

She shrugged, heading for the door. "Maybe, but it shouldn't be my boss."

"Your boss?" he roared, right on her heels. In the middle of the living room now, he grabbed her upper arm again, wheeling her around with a momentum that brought her up against his chest. Furious, she planted her palms on his shoulders and pushed free. "We made love last night, Charlotte! I'm in love with you!"

"Oh, Jake." She injected a pitying note in her voice

because she knew it would infuriate him. "Save it for the barista. Maybe she'll believe you'd fall in love with her after just a few weeks."

He flinched and then stilled.

They watched each other for several raw beats. Then, finally, he spoke.

"You think I tell every woman I've had sex with that I love her?" His voice was deathly quiet.

"Don't you?"

"No. I've never been in love before."

"Then how do you know you are now, Jake?"

He stared at her, his expression unreadable. "I just know."

"You just know," she scoffed. "Well, you'll have to forgive me if I don't want to subject me and my son to your first love. Why don't you practice for a while first? Maybe put some training wheels on it until you get the hang of it."

She'd gone too far, and she knew it.

Looking murderous, Jake grabbed her by both arms this time, yanking her up on her tiptoes until they were right in each other's faces, and there was no getting loose even if she'd had the courage to try.

"You know what I think, sweet Charlotte?" he asked, and the light in his eyes was taunting. Wicked. Knowing. "I think that last night, and the possibility of me loving you and you loving me and us building a life together with Harry scares you to death."

This sliced away several layers of her bullshit, leaving her bared to the bone.

Roger hadn't wanted her. Not really, not forever. Why would Jake?

"So you're lashing out," Jake continued. "You want to hurt me before I hurt you. Don't you?"

Snarling, she broke free or he let her go—she couldn't tell which.

"I don't have time for this!" she screeched. "You need to get dressed and leave so I can get to the hospital!"

"I'll drive you," he said grimly, looking around the floor for his clothes. "I don't want you behind the wheel when you're this upset. It's not safe for you. Or Harry," he added, playing his trump card. "Don't you agree?"

She looked away, fighting tears and loving him as much as she hated him.

Pivoting, Jake plowed into someone, hard, and heard a body thud to the ground in a cursing tangle of arms and legs. He didn't care. Grabbing the basketball, he took two running steps and dunked it in a spectacular move that left the pole swaying dangerously. Soaking wet with sweat running down his forehead and stinging his eyes, he looked around, ready for more.

"Let's go," he snapped. "What's the holdup?"

The gang—his brothers Marcus and Tony, and his cousins Harper, Shawn and Benjamin—rimmed the edge of Integrity's court, giving him a wide berth and glaring. There were also a few angry mutters, although he didn't try too hard to listen because he didn't care who said what.

He didn't care about anything, and hadn't since the

other day, when he had dropped Charlotte off at the hospital and she had dropped out of his life. Possibly for good. The only bright spot was that her mother had only suffered a bout of angina that was cured with a medication tweak. But he hadn't seen or talked to Charlotte, and the longer he went without that contact, the more unglued he became. This, naturally, led to aggression.

Hence, the bloodthirsty game of hoops.

Only none of his boys looked like they wanted to play anymore.

They were all sweaty and all roughed up to one degree or another thanks to the unusually hot September. Benji, he realized for the first time, had a nasty elbow scrape. Shawn was favoring his left ankle. There was a rip in the sleeve of Tony's T-shirt, and Harper—

"Oh, shit," Jake muttered.

Harper was down on all fours, swiping at a nose that was bleeding like a stuck pig. A surge of guilt nailed Jake the way he'd just nailed Harper, and it wasn't pretty.

He held out a hand to help him up. "Sorry, Harp. I didn't mean—"

Harper surged to his feet and kept coming, charging into Jake with a low growl.

"I'm sick of your shit, man," Harper shouted. "What the hell is your problem?"

This time, Jake was the one who went sprawling, landing flat on his back with Harper's knee in his chest.

The urge was there to fight. Though he and Harper weren't exactly BFFs, they'd never come to blows before, but he was happy to start now. On the other hand, maybe he should just let Harper beat the crap out of him. Maybe that would clear his head a little and help him think straight where Charlotte was concerned.

But the boys had other ideas, and they all piled on, pulling a snarling Harper off Jake. Tony and Marcus held Harper back. Shawn and Benji yanked Jake to his feet.

Jake and Harper glared at each other for a couple seething seconds. All of the men panted and wiped their sweaty faces on the bottoms of their shirts. Tony spoke first.

"I'm going to go out on a limb," he said, "and say that this fun little game of three-on-three is officially over. Unless we're playing to the death these days. Objections?"

Everyone grunted.

"Good." Nodding with grim satisfaction, Tony turned and headed up the hedge-lined path toward the house. "Let's get a beer. Assuming Mom'll let us in the house. Ben smells like a used jockstrap."

"Screw you, man," Benji said, laughing.

"Kindly deposit twenty dollars in my jar on the kitchen counter," said a female voice.

Jake looked around in time to see his mother emerge from the path and edge around the men, her nose crinkled against the smell of all that sweaty testosterone. In a pretty red dress and heels, even though it was Saturday, she looked like a sparkling ruby amid a handful of gravel.

"And kindly make sure you hooligans—"

"Jake's a hooligan," Shawn interjected. "The rest of us are ruffians."

"—wash your hands before you touch anything in my clean kitchen, okay?" Mama continued, a dimple appearing in one stern cheek. "Thank yooouuu."

Jake turned back to Harper. "Sorry, man. Didn't mean to rough you up like that."

Eyeballing his aunt, Harper lowered his voice and leaned into Jake's face. "Get your shit straight, JJ—"

"And I'll have a twenty from you, Harper. I take checks. Thank yooouuu."

Harper grimaced and said to Jake, "It's not our fault you hit a rough patch with your pretty paralegal, you feel me?"

Jake's jaw dropped. And here he had thought he'd been so low-key about his feelings for Charlotte. "How did you know?"

"Please." Harper ran his forearm under his dripping nose. "I have a nose like a bloodhound. The way you were looking at her at the photo shoot wasn't exactly discreet, was it? And building an office nursery, once you started eyeballing an employee with a kid? That was a clue."

With that, Harper turned to his aunt, adopting an oily smile and a sickeningly sweet tone. "Aunt Jeanette, Jake pushed me down and made my nose bleed. I think you should punish him."

Jeanette, who'd always had a soft spot for Harper, grinned indulgently and patted his cheek.

Jake rolled his eyes and made gagging sounds.

"Poor Harper," she said with a sidelong grin at Jake. "How should I punish my awful son?"

"Make him pay my fine." Harper paused, considering. "And don't give him any cookies. He'll hate that."

"Good idea," she agreed. "You run into the house and eat Jake's portion of any desserts you can find. I'm going to stay out here and give Jake a smack down. Does that make you happy?"

"Yes, ma'am," Harper said with an angelic smile. He turned toward the house and Jake turned up the volume on his gagging. Harper was really laying it on thick today. "Love you, Aunt Jeanette," Harper added, disappearing down the path.

"Love you, too," she called before turning to Jake. "I brought you some M&M's."

"Thanks. I'm not hungry."

Mama fixed him with a shocked look, as though she'd just realized how dire the situation was. "Okay. What's gotten into you, young man?"

He opened his mouth to issue the obligatory denial because grown men didn't cry on their mother's shoulders when they got their hearts trampled.

And then it hit him: Why bother?

What kind of fool would he have to be to turn away from help when help was offered? Especially when said help might help him get Charlotte back?

All of this struggle seemed to play out on his face, because Mama was giving him a kindly smile now, the type he hadn't seen since he got cut from the sixth-grade football team.

"It's about Charlotte the paralegal, isn't it?"

Jeez.

Exactly how obvious had he been with the staring on the day of the photo shoot?

"Uh, yeah." He grabbed a towel from the bench at one side of the court, covering up his too-hot face on the pretext of wiping sweat.

"Is she after your money?"

He yanked down the towel. "What? No!"

"Pregnant?"

"No, Mama." After a quick hesitation, he decided to lay it all out there and get it over with. "But she does have a son. He's two."

"Oh, that's right," Mama said glumly, rubbing her forehead with a manicured hand.

Jake shot her a withering look.

"Well, what's the problem, then?" Mama asked when she'd digested this bombshell.

"My, uh, extensive history with women has come back to bite me in the ass," he admitted.

Mama scowled, raised an index finger and opened her mouth.

"Okay, see, the thing is," he snapped, cutting her off before she got started, "I've had my guts ripped out. Right now, they feel like they've been stomped by a herd of elephants. So maybe you could give me a special twenty-four-hour exemption from putting money into your language jar. How would that be?"

Upon further reflection, Mama shut her mouth and put down her finger.

"How serious are you about this woman, Jacob?" she asked after a minute.

Jake slumped onto the bench and rested his elbows on his knees. Sudden exhaustion made him hang his head. Every blink these past several days felt like it was taking a day off his life.

What if he couldn't get Charlotte to trust in him?

What if it was really over?

Raising his head finally, he gave Mama as much of a rueful smile as he could manage. "Really? You have to ask?"

"And the boy," Mama continued. "You know what you're taking on there?"

Dumb question, Jake thought, shrugging. "No. I don't know. Does anyone ever know what they're signing up for when they have kids?"

"Jacob," she began.

"But I'm willing, Mama. For Charlotte and Harry, I'd do anything."

Mama hesitated and then nodded, satisfied. "Then you need to convince her."

"How?" he snapped. "Every time I start to make progress, some woman from my past pops up. They're like weeds."

Mama patted his cheek. If he didn't know better, he'd say there was a little affection there.

"You'll figure it out," she told him.

This was the advice for which he'd just spilled his darkest secrets? *You'll figure it out?* Seriously?

"I think you're giving me far too much credit," he said.

Mama smiled. "I disagree. What's got you so scared? Don't bother denying it."

Jake struggled, trying to put it into words. "She deserves a great man, Mama. What if it's not me?"

"It is you." The sudden urgency in her voice surprised and encouraged him. "If she doesn't see that, then she's not worthy of you. And if you don't give her time enough to grow to trust you and your intentions, then you're not worthy of her."

Jake thought about that for a minute. This, finally, sounded like advice worth following.

Could Mama be right?

"Of course I'm right," Mama told him, reading his mind and tugging his hand. "Now come inside. I have something to give you. I think it'll come in handy."

Chapter 11

"Mama, I really wish you'd sit down and rest for a minute," Charlotte said that Saturday, six mornings after her mother's trip to the hospital. "You had a heart issue this week. You are not twenty years old anymore. Stop acting like Wonder Woman."

"Hush up, girl," Mama snapped, continuing with her mixing and not bothering to look at Charlotte. "I'm working on these cupcakes with Harry. You worry about your own self."

Harry slapped his hands over his mouth and giggled. "Grammy told you to hush up, Mommy! That's funny!"

Rolling her eyes at this scene of domestic bliss in her kitchen, Charlotte turned back to her books and wished she could toss them all in the garbage. She was

ensconced in her usual place at the kitchen table, trying to get some reading done for class tomorrow. The
reading would go a whole lot faster if she wasn't mad
at the world and didn't see Jake's face everywhere she
looked. After about an hour of flipping through pages,
all she'd accomplished was…nothing. The man had her
brain in a choke hold, her heart in a sling and her gut
tied up in knots.

She was, in other words, a pathetic mess.

"I want to lick the icing!" Harry said.

"In a minute," Mama replied. "I'm not finished with
it."

"Don't use it all up!"

Mama laughed. "I'll save you some."

Charlotte put her elbows on the table and rested her
tired head on her hands. After a minute of this, she
rubbed her face, hard, wishing she could wipe away
her features and start clean. When keeping herself up-
right became too much effort, she slid her arms out of
the way and slumped across her books, lapsing into a
Jake-induced stupor.

"What's wrong with Mommy?" Harry asked in a
stage whisper.

"Oh, she's just a little lovesick," Mama said reassur-
ingly. Charlotte had made the tragic mistake of con-
fiding in her earlier, before Harry woke up. "She'll be
okay."

Lovesick.

Love.

Yeah, Charlotte thought, ignoring the way the spirals in her notebook cut across her cheek, that about covered it.

She'd fallen in love with her boss, the player.

Brilliant move, girl.

It was true, though. Who wouldn't love him?

No other man was as [INSERT ONE] as Jake:

Smart.

Sexy.

Funny.

Handsome.

Thoughtful.

Caring.

And did she mention sexy? As in, her body was still humming from the sheer joy of making love with him?

She'd taken several days off to be with Mama following her health scare, which meant she hadn't seen Jake. Nor had she taken his phone calls or answered his texts. The result was that she missed him the way she'd miss her heart if it stopped beating. Even so, as much as she wanted to throw herself into his arms again and try to see if they could make a relationship work, she didn't see how they could get there from here.

She was a mother with a young son to raise and protect, and no time for drama.

A man like Jake knew nothing about committed relationships and was a magnet for women.

Ergo, drama. So what the hell was she going to do?

There was a knock on the door.

"Someone's here, Mommy!"

Charlotte lay where she was, too emotionally wrung out to move.

Several beats went by. The person knocked again.

"Why don't I get that?" Mama muttered drily, marching out from the kitchen and tapping Charlotte upside the head as she passed the table. "I wasn't doing anything anyway."

Charlotte ignored the abuse and the snarky comment.

The door opened.

"Hello," sang a female voice.

Charlotte popped up, her pulse thundering. She knew that voice!

"I'm Jeanette Hamilton. You must be Charlotte's mother. Nice to meet you."

"You, too," Mama replied, sounding nonplussed. "Come in."

Oh, God.

Charlotte leaped to her feet, wishing she'd bothered to shower today and change into something other than the old tank top and shorts she'd slept in last night, because what if she smelled? This led to wishing that she'd also combed her hair, dabbed on some lip gloss and run the vacuum.

See? That was what lovesickness did to a person— made them into a depressed slob. Could hoarding be far behind?

Mrs. Hamilton sailed into view from the foyer, slinging a quilted black Chanel bag that probably cost Charlotte's monthly salary and looking as though she'd just stepped out of the pages of *Town & Country*. Even though she was dressed in fresh tennis whites, her hair and makeup were done, which meant either that she never went out in public without being fully put together, or her body didn't dare sweat.

Charlotte was betting on the latter.

"Hello, Mrs. Hamilton," she said, swiping a hand through her hair. "How are you?"

"Good Lord, you're a disaster." Mrs. Hamilton's gaze swept up and down her with open dismay. "I'm not sure who looks worse, you or Jake. Probably you. You look like a Depression-era street urchin."

Charlotte blinked, certain she was hallucinating. "Welcome to my home."

Harry, who was sporting a huge smudge of chocolate cupcake batter across his mouth and jaw, crept out of the kitchen and over to Charlotte's side, eyes wide.

Mrs. Hamilton bent at the waist and stared into his little face. "You must be the toddler in question," she told him.

"I'm Harry," he said, taking Charlotte's hand and hiding behind her leg.

"Harry, I'm Mrs. Hamilton," the woman said, extending her hand. "Shake."

Harry hesitantly stuck out his hand.

"Harry, your handshake is very limp," Mrs. Hamilton pronounced. "I want you to work on that."

"I'm only two," Harry said. "And a half."

"That's no excuse. What's on your face?"

"Icing."

Mrs. Hamilton straightened and looked into the

kitchen before installing herself on the sofa and cross-ing her toned legs. "Are those cupcakes? I'd love one. Maybe with a glass of milk, but only if you have whole milk. None of that skim almond soy nonsense for me. Harry, you'd better go wash your face."

Charlotte and her mother gaped at Mrs. Hamilton be-fore Mama recovered enough to hurry into the kitchen.

Harry, muttering darkly, headed for the powder room.

"But I can't stay for long," Mrs. Hamilton contin-ued. "I just came to tell Charlotte a couple things about Jake."

Charlotte, now feeling numb, sat in the nearest arm-chair. "What is it?"

"You're making him sick, dear. Do you understand that?"

Charlotte shook her head automatically. "I don't—"

"He's a fine man and he's crazy in love with you. Do you want to throw all that away?"

Deep inside her chest, Charlotte's heart started to thud with a wild hope. "I'm not sure—"

"You're worried because he's been with lots of women." She glanced up at Charlotte's mother who handed her a plate and a glass. "Thank you, dear. This is whole milk, right? Oh, and I was hoping for a few more sprinkles on my cupcake. And a fork, too, please. I don't want to get chocolate smudges on the whites be-fore my lesson."

Mama, looking dazed, took the cupcake back into the kitchen.

Mrs. Hamilton turned back to Charlotte. "Guess how many women Jake has brought home to Integrity. Go on. Guess."

"Three thousand?"

"None!"

"None," Charlotte said with disbelief.

"None," Mrs. Hamilton said flatly.

"None?"

"Is there an echo in here? Yes, Charlotte. *None.* So as soon as he brought you to the photo shoot and I saw the way he looked at you, I knew something serious was going on."

Charlotte tried to process this stunning revelation.

"He's committed to being a positive force in your boy's life. He's crazy about Harry. For goodness' sake, he built a nursery at the office because you needed one."

Charlotte struggled to regulate her breathing, willing this to be true.

"You're not after his money, are you, dear?"

"What? No!"

"Well, do you love him or not? Either you know or you don't."

"I—"

Charlotte could barely admit it to herself, much less say it aloud under Mrs. Hamilton's eagle-eyed gaze. But there was no way to stop her face from going up in flames.

"Are you going to let this chance pass you by just because Jake went through a couple of women before he met you?"

"No," Charlotte said, even though the idea of facing Jake—of trusting him with her heart—nearly made her hyperventilate.

"Well," Mrs. Hamilton said, nodding with satisfaction. "I think I have my answer, don't I? The only question now is, what are you going to do about it?" The business portion of her visit apparently concluded, she twisted at the waist and peered into the kitchen to check on the progress of her cupcake. "How are you coming with my sprinkles, dear?"

Jake knocked on Charlotte's door at eight-thirty that night.

His hands were shaking.

His mother's pep talk earlier in the day had given him enough courage to galvanize him into action, but not enough, unfortunately, to make what he was about to do any easier.

What had he told Charlotte his motto was? Go big or go home? Well, he was either about to win the gold medal in life or go down in flames.

There was no middle ground that he could see.

He hated to knock again, not wanting to wake Harry, but he had no choice—

His cell phone rang in his pocket, startling him.

Then the door swung open, revealing Charlotte, with her phone pressed to her ear.

"Hey," she breathed, eyes widening with surprise. "I was just calling you."

Jake stared at her, trying to decide whether this was

good news and hoping another ounce of courage would kick in soon. He was unspeakably grateful to see her again and felt as though he could get air all the way into his lungs for the first time in years. But she looked terrible in her shorts and T-shirt, with dark-smudged eyes and a haggard look to her cheeks that were in stark contrast to the sensual smiles she'd given him the other night when they had made love.

She hung up, lowering the phone. "What're you doing here?"

"Can I come in?"

"Of course," she said quickly, stepping aside to let him pass. "Sorry."

He took a few steps toward the sofa and then decided, screw it.

He'd had a whole scenario worked out. He'd talk calmly and logically to her. He'd argue his case. He'd drop to one knee.

All of that went out the window as he turned to face her.

"Charlotte—"

"Jake—"

Was she about to give him a final kick to the curb? What if he didn't give her the chance?

"I have to say this," he said quickly, and she closed her mouth again. "Please."

She nodded and stilled, waiting.

Great. He had the floor. Now what?

He scrubbed a hand over his nape and wrestled his thoughts into submission.

"I'm a logical guy, Charlotte." He took a gulp of air and paused to clear some of the frogs from his throat. "I analyze things. I think them through. I make plans and strategies."

She nodded again.

"So I can't explain what happened to me when I looked into your face at Starbucks. I don't have any reference points for it. All I know is that, since then, every thought I've had has been about you. Everything I've done has been for you. The promotion. The nursery at work. The toys at the barbecue. Every single time my heart has beat since then, it's been for you."

"Jake," she began, tears shimmering in her eyes.

He held up a hand to stop her. "Let me finish."

She pressed a hand between her breasts and made a sound that was equal parts laugh and sob. "I'm not sure I can take any more."

Wait...that was good, right?

He kept going because he was afraid he'd lose momentum if he stopped to find out.

"Do I have a long history with women? Yes. Do I have practice with love? No. Am I a good risk on paper?" He shrugged, raising his hands in a helpless gesture. "Probably not."

Something that looked like fear widened her eyes. "Are you dumping me?"

As if.

"I'm telling you," he said, taking a step closer, "that if you take a chance on me, I will love and protect you and Harry the way no one ever has before or ever will."

"Oh, my God," she said, openly crying now with a hand covering her mouth.

So...yeah. That was all he had.

"I'm going to go now." He moved toward the door. "I know you need time to think about—"

She recovered quickly, lowering her hand and blessing him with a smile so joyous and vibrant it was as though he'd discovered sunshine after a lifetime of cave dwelling.

"I don't need to think about anything." She put a hand on his arm, freezing him in place. "You were right. I was scared."

"I— What?" he asked, hoping she'd repeat it because he was afraid to trust his ears.

"I'm so in love with you," she said ruefully, swiping at her eyes. "I can't even see straight."

He couldn't speak, not with his heart swelling out of his chest and into his throat.

"Please don't break my heart." Charlotte stepped forward into his waiting arms. "I'm trusting you."

With a choked cry of relief, he swept her up to her tiptoes and tight against his chest, nuzzling his lips into the tender curve where her neck met her shoulder. The scent of her—freshly clean, with a hint of flowers—shot straight to his head in an intoxicating wave, and he clung to her.

Charlotte. His woman. His life.

"Is it too soon to ask you to marry me?" he wondered.

"Absolutely not."

"Good. Because my mother gave me my grandmother's engagement ring to give to you, and it's burning a hole in my pocket."

With that, he dropped to one knee, pulled out the black velvet box and opened it.

"Wait, *now?*" she cried, clapping her hands over her mouth.

"I can't wait." The confession choked him up a little, but if there was ever a time for absolute honesty in his life, this was it. Clearing his throat and blinking back the burn in his eyes, he continued. "Ever since I saw you in Starbucks, I couldn't wait—to see you again. To hear you laugh. To make love with you." He paused, emotion getting the best of him. "To start our life together. So I'm really hoping you'll marry me."

Eyes glittering with tears, she lowered her hands and nodded. "Yes. Yes. Yes!"

He surged to his feet, catching her as she flung herself at him, and they swayed together, laughing and kissing until he finally pried her left hand loose and worked the ring onto her finger.

It was a perfect fit.

"Oh, my God," she gasped, examining it from every angle. "It's art deco. Platinum. It's gorgeous."

He supposed. The details of the ring didn't interest him much, as long as Charlotte was wearing it, but his mother had told him it was a flawless three-carat diamond. And Charlotte was happy, which was all that mattered to him.

"You're gorgeous." He leaned in for another kiss, but

stopped when he spotted movement out of the corner of his eye. Turning, he saw Harry hiding in the hall. "Hey, buddy. What're you doing? Aren't you supposed to be in bed?"

Belatedly realizing that he was pretty much mauling the boy's mother right in front of him, Jake let Charlotte go and watched as Harry crept around the corner. He had on some short blue pajamas and carried Jeremy the doll pressed to his chest.

The boy's eyes were wide and curious, his steps cautious. "Jake," he said, pulling his thumb out of his mouth, "do you know how to get rid of monsters?"

Jake had been fearing some sort of birds and bees question about why he was kissing Mommy, or some such, but this was just as tricky. Reaching out, he grabbed Charlotte's hand, and she gave him a supportive squeeze.

"Uh, monsters? I'm not sure, but I can try."

"They're under my bed," Harry informed him solemnly.

"Well, let's, uh, take a look." It was too soon to drop the whole engagement thing on the little guy, he knew, but he did feel like he needed some sort of permission. It was only fair to get Harry's input, right? His life was about to change, too. "Hey, uh, Harry? Do you mind if I spend some more time here with you and your mommy? And you guys spend more time at my house? Do you think that would be okay?"

Harry tipped his head, considering. "Can I feed your shark?"

"That can be arranged," Jake said, matching his serious tone.

Harry shrugged. "Okay." He raised his hands to Jake. "Up."

Jake shot a quick glance at Charlotte, who smiled and nodded encouragingly.

And Jake, who'd never suspected that his promise to protect these two would be tested quite so soon, scooped up Harry and settled him on one side, pulled Charlotte close on the other and walked down the hall to Harry's bedroom, ready to handle any monsters that threatened his new family.

* * * * *

A brand-new miniseries
featuring fan-favorite authors!

THE HAMILTONS  *Laws of Love*
Family. Justice. Passion.

Ann Christopher	Pamela Yaye	Jacquelin Thomas
	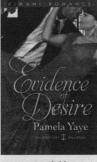	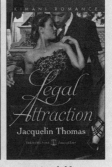
Available September 2012	*Available October 2012*	*Available November 2012*

REQUEST YOUR FREE BOOKS!

2 FREE NOVELS
PLUS 2 *FREE GIFTS!*

KIMANI™
ROMANCE

Love's ultimate destination!

Can he be her
everything when
he's not the man
she thinks he is?

Formula
for PASSION

YAHRAH
ST. JOHN

KIMANI ROMANCE

KIMANI
HOTTIES
WILL YOU MARRY ME?

Formula
for PASSION

YAHRAH ST. JOHN

As the face of her family's cosmetics empire, Courtney Adams has a
schedule that leaves no time for pleasure. But her latest commercial
shoot takes her to the Dominican Republic, where she encounters a sexy
stranger. Alone with Courtney in their exotic idyll, Jasper Jackson can't get
enough—and when a family emergency sends Courtney rushing home, he
knows he can't let her go alone....

KIMANI
HOTTIES
WILL YOU MARRY ME? +

It's All About Our Men

"This book...easily stands out from other romance novels."
—*RT Book Reviews* on *Two to Tango*

H HARLEQUIN®
™ www.Harlequin.com

Available September 2012
wherever books are sold!

KPYSJ2750912

The past could destroy their love...or fuel an unquenchable passion!

Essence
Bestselling Author

GWYNNE FORSTER

AGAINST *All* ODDS

Struggling to keep her corporate-recruiting firm afloat, Manhattan executive Melissa Grant has no time for love. Then Adam Roundtree walks into her life. But the charismatic businessman is no ordinary client. He's the man who can bring Melissa's career—and her heart—to life... until a shocking discovery jeopardizes their blossoming relationship.

> "Gwynne Forster has penned another extraordinary romance that will grip the reader with its drama, suspense and passion."
> —*RT Book Reviews* on *AGAINST ALL ODDS*

Available August 2012 wherever books are sold!

www.Harlequin.com

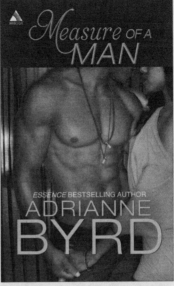

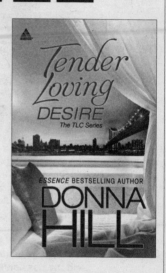
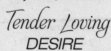